In the Jaws of Danger . . .

Jax crouched and opened the grate away from the wall like a door. Behind the grate was a safe embedded in the wall. "Memorize this combination," he said to the Hardys. Then he turned and opened the safe and put the tooth in its container inside.

"Just so you guys know," he said, turning to the Hardys. "In case anything happens to me, this is where I keep the Molar Mike. All the manufacturing schematics, test records, reports, and documentation are in here too."

"Hey, Jax, what are you talking about?" Frank asked. "What do you mean, in case something happens to you? Have you been threatened?"

"Let's get everyone out of the conference room," Jax said. "Then we can talk."

D0958357

The Hardy Boys
Mystery Stories

Available from ALADDIN Paperbacks

THE **HARDY BOYS**®

#184

THE DANGEROUS TRANSMISSION

FRANKLIN W. DIXON

SWEETWATER COUNTY LIBRARY
Sweetwater County Library System
Green River, Wyoming

Aladdin Paperbacks
New York London Toronto Sydney

If you purchased this book without a cover, you should be aware that
this book is stolen property. It was reported as "unsold and destroyed"
to the publisher, and neither the author nor the
publisher has received any payment for this "stripped book."

This book is a work of fiction. Any references to historical events,
real people, or real locales are used fictitiously. Other names, characters, places,
and incidents are the product of the author's imagination,
and any resemblance to actual events or locales or persons, living or dead,
is entirely coincidental.

First Aladdin Paperbacks edition April 2004
Copyright © 2004 by Simon & Schuster, Inc.

ALADDIN PAPERBACKS
An imprint of Simon & Schuster
Children's Publishing Division
1230 Avenue of the Americas
New York, NY 10020

All rights reserved, including the right of
reproduction in whole or in part in any form.

The text of this book was set in New Caledonia.

Printed in the United States of America
2 4 6 8 10 9 7 5 3 1

THE HARDY BOYS MYSTERY STORIES is a trademark of Simon & Schuster, Inc.

THE HARDY BOYS and colophon are registered trademarks of Simon & Schuster, Inc.

Library of Congress Control Number 2003108867

ISBN 0-689-86378-0

Contents

THE DANGEROUS
TRANSMISSION

1 Danger in the Tower

Frank Hardy stopped in front of the Bloody Tower and looked up. A shifty London fog completely obliterated any sign of the moon. In the distance he could hear a bell chime ten o'clock. The damp, musty smell of the swamp surrounding Traitor's Gate wormed its way into Frank's nose and made him sneeze. Two huge ravens scuttled away and disappeared into the blackness.

"This is what I call a vacation," Joe Hardy said, running his hand through his blond, close-cropped hair. "Tromping around the grounds of the world-famous Tower of London after hours. No tourists, no crowds."

"Absolutely," Frank agreed. "We've got the whole place to ourselves."

"More or less," came a voice from the fog. "Come on, let's get inside."

The voice was Jax Brighton's. Jax had lived with the Hardy family for a semester when he went to Bayport College a few years earlier. Frank and Joe had just arrived for a vacation in London and a reunion with their old friend.

The Hardys followed Jax up the steps of an ancient stone building. The Hardys had been to London before, and they knew that the Tower of London was more than just a tower. It was actually a huge complex of buildings on the River Thames and had been both a fort against enemy armies and the home of British kings and queens.

Surrounded by a massive stone wall, the grounds contained castles, prisons, armories, museums, and lawns once used for public executions.

Jax opened the ancient door of the Medieval Palace and poked his head through. "Hello," he called. "Nick, are you here?"

"Hey, Jax." A young man with long red hair motioned them inside. "Welcome to the thirteenth century." He shot his arm out toward Frank. "I'm Nick Rooney. You're Frank, right?" he asked. His handshake was one quick pump, and then he turned to Joe. After a similar shake he bustled off into a narrow hall. "Well, come on, then," he said.

He led them into a large room with stone walls decorated with colorful banners. Overhead, wood beams divided a massive domed ceiling into a pattern of diamonds and rectangles. From the center of the geometric dome hung an enormous chandelier. A few tall work lights on poles scattered isolated bright triangles of light, leaving the rest of the space dim and shadowed.

The room was divided in half by a row of short posts and a dark red velvet rope. Behind the rope lifelike statues of men and women in elegant royal costumes sat on thrones or stood in small groups.

"This room seems smaller with all these wax figures in it," Jax said. "I still think they should have used one of the larger halls for this exhibit." He put his black bag on a small table. It looked like a cross between a doctor's bag and a bowling bag. He opened a large side pocket and took out a plastic case. Inside the case were several sets of dentures and a few individual teeth.

"They wanted to set up some of the royals here for this special exhibit," Nick said, "so tourists could see the kings and queens in the actual houses they lived in. I voted against it, but who pays any attention to me? I'm just the historical restorer, that's all. What do *I* know!"

Frank could tell that even though Nick was joking about it, he wasn't happy about being voted down. "It's cool being here when there are no crowds to deal with," Frank said, changing the subject.

3

"You can really get a close look at everything."

"I can't get over how real these figures look," Joe added.

"Go ahead," Nick said, unhooking one of the velvet rope swags. "Get as close as you want. That's Edward I, and his queen, Eleanor. They lived in this palace over seven hundred years ago."

Frank and Joe walked around the wax figures. They were amazingly lifelike—like real people frozen in position.

"Looks like this one ended up out on the Tower Green," Joe said, standing next to a headless statue of a woman. "Isn't that where some of the kings and queens were beheaded?"

"Yes, but not that one," Nick said with a grin. "Right, Jax?"

"For that queen, it is a temporary condition," Jax agreed. He reached deep into his bag and pulled out a woman's head, perfectly created out of wax, real hair, glass eyes, and false teeth.

Nick examined the mouth carefully. "Your usual masterful work," he said, clapping Jax on the shoulder. "My friend, you are the best in the business. I'm sure you're a good orthodontist, but you need to stop wasting your time on all those living patients of yours and stick with doing the teeth for wax models." He examined the head again. "What a great job," he murmured, pointing to the corners of the mouth. "It must be all your taxidermy experience."

4

"Taxidermy?" Joe said, looking closely at the detached head. "Hey, Jax, I knew your dad was a taxidermist, but you never told us you were too."

"He did those ravens," Nick said, nodding toward two large black birds standing on the stone floor near the wall.

Frank stooped to examine the stuffed birds. They were at least two feet tall and seemed to be looking right into his eyes. "These look so real, it's weird," he observed.

"I always worked with my dad in the summers when I was in school. When he died a couple of years ago, I inherited his shop and some of his clients. But I never considered making taxidermy a career. It's just sort of a hobby."

Jax put the queen's head down on a table and crouched next to Frank. "Modern-day taxidermists actually use the same stuff to make molds of animals that dentists use to make molds of teeth," Jax said. "I used that material to make a new leg for this raven. His real one had been injured."

He ran his hand over the silky black feathers. Then he stood and went back to the queen's head. "I'm not really into taxidermy much. But it's fun combining my two skills once in a while for a special historical re-creation like this."

"I remember some story about ravens and the Tower of London," Joe said.

"Right," Frank said. "There's a legend about King

Charles II. Someone warned him that if the ravens left the Tower of London, the monarchy would fall. So he ruled that there would always be ravens living here."

"And they've been here ever since," Nick said. "We keep them happy with lodging and food. Have you told your friends, Jax, that you're about to take on another career?" he added. "One that will probably make you rich and famous?"

"Not yet," Jax said. "Let's make sure this lady has a head on her shoulders first. We can talk about that later."

The Hardys watched as Jax and Nick attached the head to the wax body. Nick pulled and shaped the model's hair and tugged at the costume until no one could see that the figure had ever been anything but one solid piece. Then he stepped back for a final look.

"No head is perfect without a set of your teeth," Nick said, smiling.

After a few more adjustments to the figure, Nick took a last look around. Then he ushered the others out. Leaving the work lights on, he pulled the door shut and locked it.

"Anybody hungry?" Nick asked. "I could use a little pick-me-up. I've got sandwich stuff in my little flat in the work section."

"I can always eat," Joe said, though he didn't want to leave this enormous place. The fog had lifted a little, and more of the grounds and buildings were visible in the pale glow of the moon.

An odd assortment of buildings ringed the greens—houses made of wood and stucco, stone towers with slits for soldiers' weapons, plain brick buildings, fancy carved palaces—all stood side-by-side within the ancient wall.

"You three head toward that building at the end of this lane," Nick said. "I have to check in with the guard and tell him we've left the Palace."

By the time the Hardys and Jax had reached the building Nick had pointed to, he was waiting for them. "I circled around the back and took the shortcut," he explained. He led them inside the employees' building, unlocked a door on the third floor, and flipped on the overhead light.

Nick's quarters were part workroom, part shop, part lab, and part library. And they were all messy. Pieces of wood and stone, scraps of fabric and paper, photos, drawings, open books, and tools covered every surface. Shelves were jammed with paints, dyes, jewels, glues, pastes, and powders. He seemed to have everything he needed to restore, repair, and re-create the Tower of London.

"Whoa, what's this?" Joe asked. "Looks like Nick's gone overboard with re-creating the history of the Tower of London. He had *himself* beheaded."

On a table against the wall was an almost perfect model of Nick's head. It was perched on a pedestal and looked so real, it was a little spooky.

"More of Jax's influence," Nick called from the little kitchen in the corner. "He's taught me a lot. Until I met him, the only way I knew how to make models was with papier mâché. He showed me how to use burlap and plaster. He added that great set of teeth himself. They're better than my real ones! That head is my third try. I think I'm getting better."

"Definitely," Jax agreed, examining the head.

Somehow, in all the chaos and disorder of the room, Nick managed to put together a tray of roast beef sandwiches, chocolate cookies, and cold sodas. He cleared a table and four chairs in the corner, and motioned the Hardys and Jax to sit and dig in.

"Man, this is good," Joe said, taking a big bite of his sandwich. "I didn't realize how hungry I was. My stomach's still on American time."

Frank nodded in agreement as he gulped some soda. Then he turned to Jax. "So what's this about a new career?" he asked.

"Not really a career," Jax said. "It's just a sort of additional project. It all goes along with working with teeth."

"You're too modest," Nick said. "Gentlemen, he's adding 'inventor' to his credentials. Revolutionary inventor. Real space-age stuff."

"It's a false tooth," Jax said, "but one with a

microreceiver in it. I call it the Molar Mike."

"Wow!" Frank said. "I've read about people hearing radio and TV programs that their tooth fillings pick up."

"But this tooth has an *actual receiver* in it," Nick prompted. "So the message won't be random."

"And it can be two-way transmission," Jax said. "The person with the tooth can talk back."

"And no one can hear the messages but the guy with the tooth?" Joe said. "Whoa, that's incredible." He slid a cookie onto his plate and reached for another, but his hand stopped in midair. "Wait a minute," he said. "This would require a major trip to the dentist. You need to get a tooth hollowed out for the receiver, right?"

"Or you can have a tooth pulled and have a bridge inserted with the false tooth receiver," Nick offered with chuckle.

"People have that kind of dental work done all the time," Frank pointed out, "without having the receiver added. I can see how this could be really valuable to some people—and worth the dental work. Where would the signals come from?"

"The receiver could be rigged to take messages from a cell phone or a hand-held data device, or even directly from a computer," Jax answered.

"Who'd be a typical user?" Frank asked.

"There are lots of applications," Jax said. "It could work for anyone who needs a steady flow of information but doesn't want to mess with an earpiece or headphone."

"Like television news readers, for instance," Nick suggested. "I was a news anchor once in Brazil. I had to wear one of those earpieces so I could always be in touch with my producer and hear any late-breaking news that might come in. But the earpiece would fall out and roll down my neck."

"The receiver could also be used to pick up foreign language instant translations," Jax added.

"Another great idea," Nick agreed. "I needed that in China for a while—and had the same problem with the earpiece. Your tooth would make it easy."

"How about espionage?" Frank offered. "What would be a better way of communicating with a spy than through a device that requires no obvious wires?"

"I've got the perfect client," Joe said. "Pro football teams. Players could get instant plays from the coaches."

"I played football in university," Nick said. "And the dental work wouldn't be much of a problem. Most players are missing teeth anyway!" He grinned as he took a bite out of a cookie. "So when does the world find out about this creation?" he asked.

"As a matter of fact, I'm having a small press conference tomorrow afternoon at the flat. Just reporters from a few scientific journals to start. After I test the reception from them, I'll branch out to the bigger guys, and—"

Jax's sentence was interrupted by the sound of footsteps moving rapidly up the hall toward Nick's quarters. The sudden pounding of a fist on the door made all four of them jump to their feet. Joe's chair tumbled over behind him.

Nick hurried to the door, and the others scrambled close behind.

"Fire, Mr. Rooney," the guard yelled from the other side of the door. "Fire! In the Medieval Palace."

2 A Shocking Welcome

"Fire!" Nick exclaimed, grabbing his jacket from the chair where he'd flung it earlier. "What happened?"

"We don't know, sir," the guard said. "We just discovered it a few minutes ago. The fire crew has been summoned."

Nick and the guard raced out into the hall without looking back. Frank was on their heels.

"We're right behind you," Joe called as he and Jax took the steps two and three at a time.

They all raced across the Green, and by the time they appeared at the scene, firemen had arrived by both truck and boat. The Hardys, Jax, and Nick were allowed to stand near the Palace, but were ordered to keep a safe distance away. Frank could feel the heat from the stone walls. The Palace had been turned into a barbecue pit.

"What do you suppose happened?" Joe asked. "We were over here just an hour ago, and everything was fine."

"As soon as I can collar one of those firemen, I'm going to find out," Nick said. "Somebody's head is going to roll. There's no excuse for an accident like this."

"The building's probably going to be okay," Jax pointed out. "It's seven hundred years old—it's not the first time it's been on fire, I'm sure."

"The walls are made of really thick stone," Frank added. "And the fire crew got here fast. So it's probably not going to spread."

"But the stuff inside . . ." Joe said, saying what was on everyone's mind.

When the flames were finally extinguished, one of the members of the fire crew escorted Nick and a couple of security guards inside the building. When they emerged a few minutes later, all three had their hands over their mouths. "It's a real mess," Nick told the Hardys and Jax. His eyes were watering, and his clothes smelled like burning candles. "The guard and I have to talk to the fire chief," he sputtered between coughs. "I'll be right back."

"I'll come with you," Frank said. "I can help you describe what it was like when we left."

13

"Good idea," Jax said, nodding to Nick.

"Okay," Nick agreed. "Come on."

Frank, Nick, and a couple of Tower guards walked over to the Green, where the fire chief waited to interview them.

"I'm glad Frank volunteered to go with Nick," Jax told Joe. "I was going to suggest it anyway—I'm eager to get the full story. And I haven't had a chance to tell Nick that you are detectives yet."

"I'd like to get inside," Joe said, watching the entrance to the Palace. A few guards stood in the doorway, talking. "Let's give it a try. They probably think we're employees anyway, since we're here so late."

Joe took out a notebook and pen and strode up the stone steps. When he reached the guards, he said, "We'll be in there only a few minutes," he said, as if he belonged there. "We have to take a few notes for our report." He gave the men a brief smile and brushed on past them. Jax followed. Joe heard the guards just a few steps behind, and he could feel their gazes. But they didn't stop him from entering the Palace.

While the guards watched, Joe and Jax stepped carefully around the charred wreckage and went into the throne room. Joe actually did take a few notes about what he found so he'd be able to fill Frank in on what he saw.

"I figured we'd find this," Joe said when they

reached what had been the exhibit of kings and queens. The wax royals had melted into odd-looking shapes. Some were grotesque, and some just funny-looking. A few were still melting.

"There's my teeth," Jax pointed out, reaching down toward a set of dentures floating on flesh-colored wax.

When a guard cleared his throat in a gentle warning, Joe stopped Jax's arm from reaching any farther. "Don't touch," Joe warned his friend.

Joe continued to walk around the room. A fire-man followed, asking Joe and Jax questions about the time before the fire.

Two guards entered the room with a tall ladder. They opened it in the middle of the floor, using it to prop up the massive chandelier which now drooped on one side. As they moved the ladder around the floor to get it in the right position, they pushed a pile of clothing that had been on one of the king figures.

When the cloth was moved aside, Joe spotted a knife with a long narrow blade. He crouched to get a better view. The antique handle was covered with wax, but he clearly saw two initials: J. B.

"Is this yours?" Joe motioned Jax over. One of the guards followed.

"Ummmm . . . yes, it is," Jax said, a hint of sur-prise in his voice.

"It looks pretty valuable," Joe said to the guard.

"Let him take it, okay? He must have dropped it when we were working here earlier. You won't get anything from it but his own prints—and maybe not even that, now that it's been in this fire."

The guard nodded, and Jax put the knife in his pocket.

By the time Joe and Jax had finished looking around and had gone back outside, Frank was searching for them.

"So what did you find out?" Jax asked. "What caused the fire?"

"The fireman said it might have had something to do with one of the work lights," Frank said. "One of them was lying on its side—it might have sparked off the fire when it fell. Or there could have been a short in the wiring. The investigators are going to work all night until they come up with something. Nick's staying too, to help."

"You were in the Palace earlier with these two gentlemen?" One of the firemen was approaching Frank. "Please tell me what you remember," the fireman said. As he had done with Joe and Jax, he questioned Frank about the time before the fire started and jotted notes in a small black book.

After forty-five minutes of interrogation the guard escorted the Hardys and Jax to the Tower gate. "There's the Tube," Jax said, nodding to a sign. They walked across the street to the Tower

Hill station for the London subway, called the Underground by the British, and nicknamed the Tube. They each bought a Travelcard, which entitled them to unlimited Underground travel for one week.

Frank, Joe, and Jax walked down three long flights of steps, then took an escalator down two more. One final flight, and they were at last at the tracks for the London subway system.

"When they call this the Underground, they're not kidding," Joe said, smiling as he scanned the handy map on the wall.

"A lot of the Underground stations were bomb shelters during World War II," Jax said. "People needed to be far from the surface."

The platform was a large open area, with several tracks for trains on the left and the right. Joe could also see a second set of tracks, which handled trains going in the opposite direction. People waited for those trains on the other side of the tracks.

On the ride back to Jax's flat, Jax showed the Hardys his father's knife.

"You had a funny look on your face when I found it," Joe said. "Why?"

"I was surprised that I'd taken it to the Tower," Jax replied. "I didn't use it for either the raven or the teeth. Frankly, I didn't realize it was even in my bag."

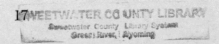
17 SWEETWATER COUNTY LIBRARY
Sweetwater County Library System
Green River, Wyoming

The Hardys and Jax got off the train at the Knightsbridge station and walked the hundreds of steps back up to the surface. A four-block walk took them to Jax's winding lane. His neighborhood was very quiet, comprising mainly narrow buildings. Most of them had shops or offices on the street level and flats on the upper floors. Jax's medical suite and two-bedroom flat were on the second floor of a brown brick building.

They walked past the two stores beneath Jax's flat. One was a jeweler's store, and the other was Jax's father's taxidermy shop. The third floor of the building was empty. Jax and the jeweler used it for storage.

"Let's go into Dad's shop," Jax said. "I'll always think of it as his, even though I own it now."

The inside of the store held a fascinating assortment of common and uncommon objects. Dozens of animals, birds, and fish hung on walls, perched on tables, and rested in display cases. Jax described the variety of animal shapes and parts that he was working on.

"Here's one made from papier mâché," he pointed out, "and one from burlap and plaster, like the head Nick made of himself. This one's made from dental compound. And some are formed from acrylic or fiberglass."

He pulled out some drawers with trays in them. "You can't preserve lips, tongues, ears, noses, or eyes," he said. "So you either make fake ones your-self or buy them ready-made."

In the back of the store was his studio. Leaves, branches, moss, rocks, and other objects to help the mounts look real sat on shelves. Tools, wire, brushes, surgical implements, and measuring instruments were scattered on tables.

Jax walked over to a large cabinet and opened the door to reveal bottles and cans of paints, dyes, and cleaning fluids. "Some of the hides have a lot of fat in them," he said, "so we use gasoline to dissolve it. Dad used arsenic to kill bugs in the furs, but most of us use borax now."

He led the Hardys to a wooden cupboard that was mounted on the wall like a medicine cabinet. Inside was a large knife rack with a cubbyhole full of sharpening stones. He pulled the knife that Joe had found from his pocket, picked off the dollops of melted wax, and slipped the blade down into the empty slot.

"The weird thing is that I never use any of the knives in this case," Jax said. "I have my own set. Taxidermists are funny about using their own knives. Dad's are pretty special to me, and I wouldn't want anything to happen to them, so I don't take them out. But I must have. I'd really hate to lose one—which I almost did. Thanks, Joe."

"This is a really unusual studio," Joe said, "but cool."

"Most of my jobs have been fun. I especially enjoy building an animal from scratch—making a form, and then fitting the hide over it. I did a really good dog for the Sherlock Holmes house. We'll go see it sometime while you're here."

Jax turned out the lights and led the Hardys out the back door of the shop and into an alley behind the building.

"You have your key, right?" Jax asked. "Go on up. I want to get the mail." While Jax continued on to the lane and toward a jumble of old-fashioned mailboxes, Frank and Joe walked to the iron stairway on the side of the building that led up to Jax's second-floor flat.

Long snakes of fog swirled through the air, alternately hiding and exposing the moon. A damp breeze riffled through Frank's open jacket. Chilled, he reached in his pants pocket for the key Jax had given him when the Hardys had arrived the day before.

Frank stood on the landing in front of the door and pushed the key into the lock. He turned it, but the key wouldn't budge.

Frank looked at his brother standing halfway down the stairs. "I think Jax gave us the wrong key," he told Joe. "This one won't—"

Wham! Frank couldn't finish his sentence before the wind was knocked out of him. The door opened behind him and slammed hard into his back.

He stumbled to one knee, then felt himself being pulled up from behind. He heard Joe call his name, but the voice sounded so far away. The last thing he saw before he blacked out was the shocked look on Joe's face.

3 Off with His Head

Joe had just a few seconds to brace himself before his brother's body sailed into him. He stood his ground long enough to maintain some control over their inevitable fall. Then Frank's head butted into him and the two tumbled back down the steps.

"What happened?" Jax yelled, sprinting over to the steps.

"Make sure Frank's okay," Joe ordered, scrambling to his feet. "Then call the police," he called back as he raced along the walk to the lane. "Someone was in your house."

When Joe got to the lane, he stopped for a minute. There was no one in sight in either direction. He strained to hear through the thick, hovering fog. He thought he heard the clicking of footsteps in the distance toward the right. *The Underground!* he thought. *Of course!*

Joe raced the four blocks to the Underground station. At each intersection he paused for a moment, listening for footsteps or the whirring of bicycle wheels or a vehicle motor. There was nothing.

He clambered down the five flights to the Underground in record time. There were a few people waiting for the train, but he saw no one familiar. He didn't recognize any of the people waiting as the person who slammed out of Jax's flat and pushed Frank down the stairs. Of course, he hadn't really seen the figure—but no one in the station looked at all suspicious. He decided to hang around there for a few minutes, though, to see if the person showed up.

A peculiar loud noise interrupted the familiar sound of subway trains coming and going. Joe looked to his left and saw a strange-looking yellow car moving by itself about two miles an hour along the track. It had no windows or doors. "What kind of car is that?" he asked an Underground security guard who was also watching it.

"It's our new tunnel cleaning train," the guard answered, raising his voice as the car passed by. "We're trying it out. It takes in about two million pounds of trash and garbage a day."

"What's the most unusual thing it ever picked up?" Joe asked.

"I never saw it myself, but I hear we got a mattress once," the guard said, shrugging. "But mostly, lots of umbrellas, cell phones, garbage, and clothing."

Joe waited and watched the platform for a few more minutes, then decided to return to the flat. All the way back, he kept his senses alert, watching and listening for a sign that the intruder was still nearby.

While Joe was tracking the intruder, Frank and Jax checked out the flat. At first Frank felt a little woozy from his slamdunk to the bottom of the stairs. But he grew stronger with every step. Careful not to disturb any possible evidence, he led Jax through the living quarters and then into the medical suite.

When they got to Jax's medical lab, Frank stopped. "Where do you keep your invention—the Molar Mike?" he asked.

"It's in my medical office," Jax answered.

Jax started toward the office. As Frank followed, he noticed something glimmering on the floor. "Just a minute," he called out. He walked over and crouched near where he'd seen the glow. A piece of gray metal lay on the floor.

"It's shaped like part of a leaf," Jax observed, crouching down with Frank.

Frank reached for a tissue off the lab counter. Then he used it like a glove to turn the piece of metal over. "There's part of a hinge on one end," he said. "It might be half of a clasp. Have you ever seen this before?"

"Never," Jax said.

"Do you have a camera in here?" Frank asked.

"Sure," Jax said. "It's one of those instant ones." He went to a closet, got the camera, and brought it over.

"Perfect," Frank said. He took one shot of the front of the pewter fragment, and another of the back. Then he folded the tissue over the metal and slipped the package into an envelope.

While Frank took the pictures, Jax went into his office. "The Molar Mike's still there," he reported, quickly returning to the lab.

Frank heard the police car, and he and Jax went to the door. Joe arrived at the same time.

"You okay?" Joe asked his brother. "We took quite a roll out there."

"I don't even remember it," Frank said. "I got slammed from behind, and then I blacked out, I guess. What happened exactly? Someone was inside the flat?"

"Until you started to open the door," Joe said, nodding.

"Right," Frank said. He thought back to the moment at the top of the steps. "Now I remember. I tried to turn the key, but it wouldn't budge."

"The person inside was probably jamming the

25

lock," Joe pointed out. "Then he—or she—came barreling out, knocked into you, Frank, and shoved you down the stairs into me. We both ended up on the ground. The intruder jumped over the stair railing and ran off. I took off after him but lost the person's trail in the Underground."

"Can you describe the person any better?" the policeman asked, introducing himself as Officer Somerset.

"Well, I didn't get a really good look," Joe said. "I think it was a man—but it could have been a woman, I guess. Pretty athletic. He dropped from the landing over the stairway, and took right off. Outran me for several blocks."

"How about clothing?" the officer prompted.

"Dark pants and jacket, black cap with a little brim on the front . . . I couldn't see any hair." Joe stopped for a moment to think back. "Medium build," he continued, "a few inches less than six feet tall, maybe."

"This person didn't speak?" the policeman asked.

"No," Joe said, shaking his head. "Have you had a chance to look around?" he asked Jax. "Is anything missing?"

"Not that I've discovered," Jax said.

"I found something," Frank said. He reached inside the envelope, pulled out the lumpy piece of tissue, and peeled back the ends of the paper to reveal the small piece of pewter.

"It could be a piece of jewelry or an ornament of some kind," the policeman suggested. Frank refolded the package and put it back in the envelope. Then he handed it to the officer.

Frank, Joe, Jax, and the policeman made another quick tour of the flat but found nothing else. "Let me know if you discover anything missing or find anything suspicious," the policeman told Jax, handing him a card with a telephone number.

After the officer left, the Hardys helped Jax make one more security check around the second floor. They checked all door and window locks.

When the Hardys finally hit the beds in Jax's guest room, it was two o'clock in the morning. Frank was still wired from the day's excitement. "Looks like this is going to be a working vacation," he said to Joe.

"Are you talking about the fire at the Tower or the break-in here?" Joe asked.

"The break-in," Frank said. "It looks like the fire could've been an accident. I'm not sure why anyone would burn the exhibit. But I can see why someone might rob Jax, can't you?"

"You're talking about the Molar Mike, right?" Joe guessed.

"You got it," Frank answered. "That thing's rigged so people can get messages from a computer or a cell phone. It opens up all sorts of possibilities."

"Uh huh," Joe agreed. "For good and bad. If

someone can program a computer to communicate with a tooth receiver—"

"Someone else can hack in and change the program," Frank said, finishing his brother's sentence.

"Exactly."

"That pewter piece might help us," Frank pointed out. "I took a photo of it before the policeman got here."

Joe heard the rhythmic breathing that told him his brother was falling asleep.

Joe turned over and tried to get his mind to shut down. As he finally felt sleep coming on, a peculiar sound reached his ears.

Joe fought back the drowsiness and turned on his back. *Skrrrrt. Skrrrrt.* The odd sound drifted through the air again. *It's like a scraping noise,* Joe thought. *And it's coming from up there.* He looked at the ceiling. When he heard the sound again, he reached over and punched Frank's bed.

"Wake up," he whispered. "Frank! Wake up."

"Mmmmmmmm, this better be good. What's up?"

"Listen," Joe whispered.

Frank sat up and shook his head.

The Hardys sat still. Joe strained to hear the sound again, but there was nothing. Then, as he turned to swing his legs out from under the blankets, he heard a thump on the ceiling.

"Whoa," Frank said. "There's something up on the third floor."

"I heard a scraping sound earlier," Joe said, his voice low. He pulled sneakers on as he talked. "There's definitely something moving around up there."

"That's supposed to be an unoccupied flat," Frank reminded his brother. "Jax told us that he and the other shopkeeper in this building use it for storage since there's no one living there. Maybe it's the jeweler, checking some of his stuff."

"At this hour?" Joe wondered. "Maybe. If it's not him, though, who—or what—could it be?" Joe asked.

"Could be just a rat or a mouse," Frank pointed out. "Or a bird that got trapped in there. Let's check it out."

The Hardys grabbed flashlights, left Jax's living quarters, and quietly moved into the medical suite. They walked through the reception area and into the hallway that led to the examination rooms. At the end of the hall was the lab and the door leading to the stairway up to the third floor.

They had to move slowly. The old building had creaky floorboards and stairs. They took each step very carefully, so as not to make any noise.

Finally they reached the top floor. It was very dark, but they could tell they were in a hallway. Frank turned on his penlight and aimed the beam at the wooden floor. He waited a minute but didn't hear anything, so he cautiously moved the light around the hall.

In the shadows he could see that at the end of the short hall stood a wooden door with a dark, frosted glass windowpane in the top half.

"There's no light in there," Frank whispered. "So it's probably not the jeweler."

Frank and Joe stepped silently down the hall toward the door. As they got closer Frank lowered his light so that it shone only on the floor. The beam reflected off the dusty floor back up to his face, causing an eerie light effect.

When he reached the door, Frank put his ear next to it, coming as close to the door as he could without actually touching it. He heard nothing and gestured that message to Joe.

Frank grasped the doorknob tightly. He focused on turning the knob slowly and silently. He wasn't surprised to find it was not locked. When he heard the latch click, he stood very still for a moment. But he heard no sound from the other side of the door.

Keeping his right hand clenched around the doorknob, he reached over with his left hand and inched the door open.

He gazed through the narrow opening into inky blackness beyond. He could feel Joe take a small gasp of air, and realized that both of them had been holding their breath. He waited for his eyes to adjust to the lack of light. Then he pushed the door open farther, and he and Joe stepped inside the dark space.

Frank sidled around the edge of the room. As his eyes became more accustomed to the darkness, he began to see shapes. A narrow glow from a distant window formed silhouettes and shadows across the room. He began to make out stacked boxes and packages and pieces of furniture. Mounted animal head shapes jutted out from the wall, and glass eyes seemed to follow the boys' movements.

Frank and Joe continued to circle the large room, staying hidden behind the stored objects. Frank concentrated on his sense of hearing, listening for the slightest sound other than the barely perceptible ones that he and Joe made.

Frank jumped a little when he felt Joe's hand pull on his arm. Then Joe stepped behind a stack of boxes, nodding his head toward the left.

Frank ducked down behind a desk chair. He focused his hearing toward the direction in which Joe had nodded.

He heard the eerie sound immediately, and it was only a few yards away. Someone—or *something*—was breathing very fast.

Frank looked over at Joe, who gave him a knowing nod. Joe gestured that he was going to circle around and try to get behind the source of the breathing.

Frank peered around from behind the chair and watched Joe's silhouette inch through the stacks and piles. He saw Joe pick up a chair leg that was leaning against a table.

For a moment the room was still. Then a bulky shape jumped out from behind a stack of cartons and lunged toward Joe.

"Joe—watch out!" Frank yelled. He clicked on his light. A man, caught in the beam, reversed his direction and swung around to face Frank. Then the man grabbed a hatbox and threw it at Frank's light.

Frank jumped back, and the hatbox crashed to the floor and popped open. Like a bowling ball headed toward a spare, the contents of the box rolled to a stop at Frank's legs. He swung the light beam down to his feet.

Smiling up at him was a human head.

4 The False Tooth?

Breathing fast, Frank tore his attention away from the head at his feet and looked up. He saw Joe's shadow—complete with the raised table leg— stand up behind a lumpy figure. Frank quickly aimed his light in that direction.

"Don't move," Joe said to the man in front of him. The light beam caught the stranger's ruddy, puffy face. Frank quickly zigzagged the light across the man's body. He was wearing a bright red-and-white workout suit. The man raised his hands, palms out, to show that he had no weapon.

Joe lowered the table leg and walked back to the door. He flipped on the overhead light, and Frank turned off his penlight and put it away.

"Who are you?" Frank asked.

"I might ask the same of you," the man fired back. He had a slight French accent.

"We are up here to investigate a trespasser," Joe said. "Answer my question: Who are you, and why are you in this room?"

The stranger looked around. "This is my storage room," he answered. "I've been doing some inventory work.

"At this time of night?" Frank asked.

"In the dark?" Joe added.

"What's going on?" Jax asked as he slammed open the door. "Pierre! What are you doing here?"

A startled look flashed across the man's face. Then he vaulted over a couple of boxes and raced for the door. Joe and Jax stepped in front of him and blocked his path. The man's face was streaked with dark red flushes. As Pierre's hands drew up into fists, Frank stepped over to join the other two.

The stranger seemed to realize he was no match for three young men, so he relaxed his stance and shrugged. Slowly the red receded from from his skin, indicating that he was beginning to calm down a little.

"Okay, let's start again, Pierre," Frank said. "What are you doing up here?"

"This is Pierre Castenet," Jax said, picking up the papier mâché head and putting it back in the hatbox. "He's a soccer coach from Toronto— semi-professional. He found out about the Molar

Mike from my Canadian manufacturer. He contacted me about having a Molar Mike made to use with his team. I turned him down, but he's been bugging me to loan him a prototype to try out."

"I'm sure you can all see what a good idea that is," Pierre said. He had a very smooth way of talking, like a salesman trying to talk you into something you really don't want to buy.

"Everyone wins," Pierre continued. "Jax learns how well his invention works in a real-life setting. And my team wins soccer games because I can tell my captain everything that is happening on the field."

"So you decided to steal the tooth," Joe said.

"No, no," Pierre said, the red creeping back into his face. "No, not at all. I would never steal it. I was here to hide out."

"Not a good answer," Joe pointed out. "Tell us what's going on, or the police can handle it."

"Very well," Pierre said. "I will tell you the truth. This is all a misunderstanding."

He adjusted his position, and then began explaining. "I came to talk to you again. I wanted to make one more appeal before returning to Canada. I have what I believe is a tantalizing offer. Your pocket will be lined with more research money."

"As far as I'm concerned, breaking into my home pretty much destroys any possibility of a deal," Jax said angrily. "Now or in the future."

35

"Just listen," Pierre pleaded. "When I arrived, your door was open, so I entered. I called your name, but there was no answer, so I figured you might be with a patient. I went into your medical suite, but you weren't there either. Since the door had been open, I reasoned that you had merely stepped out and would return soon."

Pierre slid off the desk and paced a few steps back and forth. "I decided to wait," he continued. "I admit that I poked around, looking for the Molar Mike. But I assure you, I just wanted to look at it. I was not going to steal it," he insisted.

"I was in your lab when I heard a loud commotion outside," he said. "It sounded almost like a fight. Then I heard a police car pull up. I was nervous about being in your lab and afraid no one would believe I was just waiting for you."

Pierre stopped pacing and looked at Jax. "I decided not to reveal myself. I tried to find a back way out and discovered the stairs up to this floor. I broke in and hid out. You really need to get a better lock for that door," he cautioned Jax.

"I was waiting up here until it was quiet downstairs, and then I intended to leave without disturbing you any further." Pierre shrugged his shoulders again. "But your friends here surprised me. As you can see, I am mostly innocent of any wrongdoing and would like to be on my way now."

Jax pulled the Hardys over to a corner where

they could talk privately. "What do you think?" he asked. "Do we believe him or not?"

"I don't know about his story," Joe said. "But I do know one thing: He's definitely not the person who barreled out of your house when we first got there. Pierre's much bigger than that guy."

"It's possible that when Pierre got here, the door was unlocked because the other person had already broken in," Frank added. "Pierre says he went right into your office. If he was in there and the other intruder was in your living quarters, they might not have heard each other."

"He talked about a commotion outside, like a fight," Joe said. "That definitely could have been us barreling down to the bottom of the stairway."

"Pierre actually could be valuable to us and to the police," Frank pointed out. "When he finds out another person was here at the same time, he might remember something about it. Let's try to get some information out of him."

Frank outlined his plan with Joe and Jax, and then the three of them walked back to where Pierre waited.

"Okay, here's the deal," Frank offered. "Jax won't press charges, under one condition. You said you heard a commotion—that there was possibly another intruder in the flat while you were in the medical suite. So you need to report to the police immediately—we'll tell you to whom, and where.

You must tell this officer that you were here. It's possible you might recall something that will help nail the other intruder."

"I will back your story that you were here to meet with me," Jax added. "But if you don't agree to this condition, or if we find out that you didn't go immediately to talk to this officer, I'll have you picked up. I'll press charges of breaking and entering, trespassing, and attempted theft."

"You won't have to," Pierre said. He looked relieved. "I will talk to the police immediately."

Frank pulled out the photos he'd taken earlier of the metal fragment he'd found in Jax's lab. "Have you ever seen this before?"

"What?" Pierre asked. "That metal thing?"

"Is it yours?" Frank asked.

"I don't even know what it is," Pierre said.

Frank put the photos away, and Jax escorted Pierre Castenet down to the flat. Once they'd left, the Hardys searched through the storage room but didn't find anything that seemed out of place so they joined Jax to see Pierre off.

"Do you think he'll go to the police?" Joe asked.

"I do," Jax said. "From what I understand, he has had problems with the law before, so he probably doesn't want to make any more trouble."

Jax closed the door and locked it. "I need to get some sleep," he said. "The press conference is this afternoon at one thirty. I should be slightly awake for that," he added with a grin. "You guys are going to be there too, right?"

"We wouldn't miss it," Frank assured him.

Jax and the Hardys went to their rooms and fell into their beds. This time, their sleep was not interrupted.

Thursday morning Frank and Joe showered and dressed very quickly. They both felt an urgency to get on the case. While Joe showered, Frank called Officer Somerset to make sure that Pierre Castenet had reported to the station. He had.

While Frank showered, Joe called Nick to find out if the fire in the Medieval Palace was still being considered an accident. The news was not very good.

"Well, they no longer think it was an accident," Nick said. "They're saying the wires to the work lights were cut by a very sharp instrument. They also found some gasoline. They think that was used to prime the fire."

"It's a wonder it didn't explode," Joe pointed out. "There would have been a lot more damage."

"I know. Anyway, the guard remembered the knife you found, and so they want it back for the investigation," Nick said.

"That shouldn't be a problem," Joe replied, "but Jax doesn't even remember taking it over there. It's his father's."

"They also found a wad of dental compound close to where they think the fire originated," Nick said. "I told them that it was no big deal because Jax is an orthodontist and did the teeth for all the models. I think they understood, but they still want to talk to him again. I don't think they see him as a suspect, but they're in the dark right now. So they're exploring all the possibilities, I guess—tying up the loose ends."

Nick gave Joe a phone number. "Have Jax call and set up a meeting, okay?" he asked.

"Sure," Joe said. He decided not to tell Nick about the two intruders in the flat last night until he got the okay from Jax.

"Let's keep in touch," Nick said before hanging up. "Maybe we can get together later."

After the Hardys got dressed and had a quick breakfast, they joined Jax in his lab. He was getting ready for the press conference.

"So this is the Molar Mike," Joe said, holding the tooth in his hand. "Unbelievable. It looks like a regular tooth."

"Except for this," Jax pointed out, gently pulling the tooth apart. The inside looked like a typical microelectronics setup, with chips and wires. He showed them test results, production graphs, and manufacturing schematics.

"Totally awesome," Joe said. "This would be worth a trip to the dentist."

The Hardys left the flat at about ten thirty. Their first stop was the police station to check in with Officer Somerset. He told them he had a lead. There had been some recent burglaries in the area, and Jax might have been hit by the same culprit.

Frank and Joe looked at hundreds of burglar mug shots. It was a waste of time for Frank because he hadn't gotten a good look at the man who'd shoved him from behind. Joe picked out several that fit the general look of the man he'd seen. But they all turned out to be false leads—some were in prison, others had left the country.

Officer Somerset also confirmed that Pierre Castenet had reported in—but he had remembered nothing new that might help the investigation.

After more than an hour the Hardys went to the hotel where Pierre had been staying. The reservations clerk told them he had checked out early that morning and had left no forwarding address. Frustrated, Frank and Joe returned to the flat.

Precisely at one thirty Jax began to speak. He flashed a winning smile and introduced the Molar Mike to the world for the first time. The Hardys walked to the back of the room so they wouldn't block the view of any of the journalists.

"Good afternoon, everyone," Jax began. "I'm pleased to introduce to you my revolutionary concept." His speech was accompanied by the clicks of cameras, the whirs of videocameras, and the staccato sounds of laptop computer keys. A small group had assembled to hear about the Molar Mike—about a dozen reporters and five photographers.

"Now I'd like to open the floor to questions," Jax said, concluding his formal presentation. "I'll try to answer as many as I can."

He answered questions about the mechanical and scientific workings of his invention but was careful not to reveal any of the secrets behind it. After a dozen questions Jax finally seemed to reach his limit. "Thanks again, everyone, for coming. Please be sure to get a press kit from the stack on the conference table. And don't forget to enjoy some of the delicious refreshments the caterer has pre—"

The conference room door slammed open, startling Jax enough for him to stop speaking in the middle of a word. A man shoved past reporters and the Hardys and stopped next to Jax.

"Geoffrey, I'm surprised to see you," Jax said with a thin smile.

"I'm sure you are," the man said. He looked like he was in his forties. He was of medium height and weight and had a completely bald head.

The man turned to address the others in the room. "My name is Geoffrey Halstead," he announced. "*I* am the inventor of the Molar Mike."

5 Gotcha!

"Geoffrey!" Jax said. "That's not true—and you know it."

"We'll just let the courts decide that," Geoffrey said. He nodded to the man who had accompanied him into the room. The reporters put down their refreshments and opened up their computers and notebooks. While cameras revved back up, the man handed a bulging envelope to Jax.

Jax tore open the envelope and pulled out a fat wad of papers. As he skimmed through them an astonished look spread across his face.

"Ladies and gentlemen," Geoffrey said, "I have nothing further for you today. However, I assure you that there is much more information to come about who is the rightful creator and owner of the so-called Molar Mike."

Geoffrey Halstead and the other man walked briskly back out of the room.

Jax was hammered with a new round of questions. "Look, I'm just as shocked by this as you all are," he said. "I have only one response. Geoffrey Halstead is a liar. I am the sole creator, inventor, and owner of the Molar Mike. Thank you all for coming. Enjoy the refreshments."

Jax walked back to the Hardys. Shaking his head in dismay, he handed the large envelope over to Frank.

"He's suing you?" Joe guessed.

"Yep," Jax said as Frank looked over the pages.

"Who is he?" Joe asked. "Why would he make this claim?"

"I thought he was a friend," Jax said. "He's a jeweler."

"Of course," Frank said. "I knew I recognized the name. He owns the shop on the first floor."

"That's right," Jax said. A few reporters circled around, but Joe firmly ushered them back to the refreshment table. He made it clear that there would be no more answers from Jax at that time. In groups of two and three, the press people finally began leaving the room.

Joe returned to Frank and Jax. "So what does it say?" he asked, looking quickly over the papers from Geoffrey Halstead.

"He's demanding to be declared the co-creator of the Molar Mike," Frank explained. "He wants a full financial and legal accounting, cash reparations, and a percentage of future profits."

While they talked, the Hardys helped Jax pack up the display materials and extra press kits. The tooth was packed back into its insulated container. Jax carried the container into his office. The Hardys followed with the rest of the materials.

Jax slid a file cabinet away from the wall. Behind it was what looked like an ancient heating grate—probably part of the original architecture of the hundred-year-old building.

Jax crouched and opened the grate away from the wall like a door. Behind the grate was a safe embedded in the wall. "Memorize this combination," he said to the Hardys. Then he turned and opened the safe and put the tooth in its container inside.

"Just so you guys know," he said, turning to the Hardys. "In case anything happens to me, this is where I keep the Molar Mike. All the manufacturing schematics, test records, reports, and documentation are in here too."

"Hey, Jax, what are you talking about?" Frank asked. "What do you mean, in case something happens to you? Have you been threatened?"

"Let's get everyone out of the conference room," Jax said. "Then we can talk." He slammed the safe door shut and closed the grate, completely disguising the secrets behind it.

The Hardys and Jax went back to the conference room. The rest of the journalists were gone, and the caterer had nearly finished cleaning up. The leftovers were boxed up for Jax's refrigerator, and the conference room was being cleaned and swept.

After the caterer left, Frank, Joe, and Jax took the leftovers into the kitchen of Jax's flat. They spread out some of the food on the kitchen table and sat down in front of the window. Outside a mist sprinkled down on the trees that dipped over the street.

Snacking on cheese, crackers, fruit, and cookies, the three talked about Geoffrey Halstead's lawsuit.

"Okay, Jax, tell us what's really going on here," Frank urged his friend. "You know we'll be glad to help you. But we have to know the full story."

"Geoffrey and I have been friends a while," Jax began. "We've known each other since he began leasing the shop downstairs. We're both craftsmen, and I ran some ideas by him about the general design of the Molar Mike without being specific about the actual invention. But I didn't consult with him in any official way, and I didn't use the ideas we discussed. He never really knew exactly what I was talking about."

Jax grabbed a piece of fruit. "I have a good

attorney. I'm sure he'll be able to resolve this. I'm not really worried about the lawsuit."

"What *are* you worried about?" Frank asked.

"What do you mean?" Jax answered. He seemed to be avoiding Frank's gaze.

"You said you were showing us your safe in case anything happens to you," Frank reminded him.

"So what's up with that?" Joe asked. "Is someone threatening you?"

"Yes, but I can't prove it," Jax said. "Ever since I started work on the Molar Mike, somebody's been bugging me."

"For example . . . ?" Frank prompted.

"First, this isn't the first time someone's broken into my flat. It's happened at least twice before. I also think that someone has hacked into my computer— the one with all my plans on it. I've done some major electronic searches, but I couldn't find the source."

"Sounds like someone's on the trail of your invention," Joe said.

"And there's more," Jax said. "I've been followed, and someone even tried to run me off the road once. It might have been just an accident, but I don't know. . . ."

"Can you identify any of the people who have been threatening you?" Frank asked.

"No, I have nothing," Jax said. "Help me find out what's going on, will you?"

"Absolutely," Joe answered. He took out the

number Nick had given him earlier. "You need to call them," Joe said. He repeated what Nick had said about the fire chief's investigation, and how he'd wanted to talk to Jax.

"That sounds kind of weird," Jax said, "like they think I had something to do with the fire."

"I know," Joe replied, "but Nick said they just want to interview you. He assured them you're okay."

Jax called the number and made an appointment for six o'clock. Then he called Nick and told him what was happening. The Hardys listened as Jax continued his conversation, but they couldn't make much sense out of it. Jax filled them in after he hung up.

"I told the Tower of London guard that I was bringing you two with me. Hope that's okay."

"Sure," Frank said, checking his watch. "It's a quarter to five now, so we've got about an hour."

"I asked Nick to meet us at this club not far from here," Jax said. "It's really wild. I can't wait to take you there. But he can't get there in time. He's giving a dinner speech for a youth group up in Kensington. He said to check in with him after we're finished at the Tower. Maybe we can hook up then."

"When I talked to him earlier, I didn't tell him what happened here last night," Joe said. "I wanted to check with you first. I didn't know if you wanted people to know."

"I appreciate that," Jax said. "I told him, though. He already knew about all the pressure I'd been getting from Pierre."

Frank told Jax about the Hardys' meeting with Officer Somerset. "Seems a little weird that Pierre checked out of his hotel," Joe said. "I'm sure the police told him to stick around."

Frank took out the instant photo he took of the pewter fragment they found in Jax's lab. "You're sure you don't recognize this?" he asked Jax again.

"Absolutely. I thought about it when I went to bed last night."

"Maybe a patient dropped it," Joe suggested. "Maybe a hinge broke, and this part fell to the floor, and the owner just didn't notice."

"Except none of my patients are ever in the lab," Jax pointed out. "Even if one of them got in there by mistake, I had a cleaning crew go over the place just before the break-in. I wanted it really clean for the press conference. If it had been on the floor, the cleaners would have found it."

"So it had to have been dropped after the cleaning crew left," Frank reasoned.

"Right," Jax said. "And no one was in there afterward except the person who broke in."

"And Pierre," Joe reminded them.

"But he said it wasn't his," Jax said.

"And if it was his, do you think he would have said so?" Joe asked. "What if he was in the lab looking for the tooth? He sure wouldn't want you to know that, so he'd lie about the pewter piece."

"I'd really like to talk to him again," Frank said. "Jax, do you have any idea where he might have gone after he left the hotel?"

"He was staying in a friend's apartment when he first got in touch with me a few weeks ago," Jax said. "Maybe he went there. I have the address."

"Sounds like a good place to start," Joe said.

"Let's go," Jax said. "I know right where it is. We can walk."

Frank had a creepy feeling from the minute they left the flat. He was sure they were being followed. He casually looked around once and noticed a woman about a block behind them. As soon as Frank's eyes caught hers, she stepped into a shop and out of sight. Frank noticed her trailing them again, though, a minute later.

They had walked about five blocks when Jax stopped in front of a general store. "I need to go in here for a few minutes," he said. "I won't be long."

"No problem," Joe said, following him into the store. Frank stepped inside too, but stayed near the front of the store. He was able to look through the window and get a full view back down the street.

There she is again, he noted to himself, spotting the woman. *And she's looking this way.*

Frank was sure that the woman couldn't see him

from his post inside the store. She continued to stand in front of another shop window about half a block away. But she spent most of her time sneaking looks up the street at the general store.

As Frank watched she took a cell phone from her purse. She tried to make a call but then slapped the phone a couple of times and redialed.

"What's up?" Joe asked, joining Frank.

"See that woman in the green coat?"

Joe nodded his response.

"She's been following us since we left the flat."

"It looks like her phone's not working," Joe observed.

As the Hardys watched, the woman walked to a pay phone on the corner across the street from the general store.

"This might be time for a little shoulder surfing," Joe said. He grabbed a pair of high-powered binoculars from a store display. Then he stood where he had a clear view over the woman's shoulder to the pay phone keypad.

"Okay, Frank," Joe said. "Write down these numbers. Five-five-"

The scene was trapped in the circle lenses of Joe's binoculars.

"Five-seven-"

The woman's finger paused over the number buttons.

"Three-eight-"

Then her head swiveled suddenly.

"Uh-oh."

Joe felt a chill down his spine. Through the binoculars, he saw that the woman was staring straight into his eyes.

6 Caught in the Crypt

When Joe saw the woman look into his eyes, he felt the hairs on his arms bristle. He ducked out of sight, but he knew it was too late. His pulse pounded as he looked over at Frank.

Joe knew that Frank wouldn't look in his direction because it would be better if the woman didn't know they were connected. Sure enough, Frank was pretending to read a newspaper. But although his head was bowed down toward the paper, his eyes were aimed at the pay phone and the woman standing there.

"She's still looking over here," Frank muttered out of the corner of his mouth. "Stay down."

Joe waited for what seemed like a long time but was only five minutes. Then Frank whispered again.

"She turned away," he said. "It looks like she's going to make another call. No, now she's hesitating. . . ." He snapped the newspaper shut and dropped it on a nearby bench. "That's it. She's leaving. You're all clear."

Joe stood up. The woman was walking quickly down the street toward the corner. "You go on with Jax," Frank called back as he left the store and crossed the street. "I'll catch up with you at the Tower of London."

"Where's Frank going?" Jax asked as he walked up to join Joe.

As they walked to the Underground, Joe told Jax about the woman who had been following them.

"Do you have any idea who she is?" Jax asked.

"She looks familiar to me," Joe said. "I want to check with Frank and see if he got the same impression. I think she might be a woman our Dad chased down a few years ago. We'll check her out when we get back to my computer."

They went by the flat where Pierre had been staying, but there was no one home. Jax left a note for Pierre in the door. Then they decided to walk the rest of the way to the Tower of London.

When they arrived at the Tower, it was closing. Guides dressed in knee-length black coats trimmed in yards of red stripes were ushering out the tourists. Jax gave his name to the guard posted at the gate, as he'd been instructed to do. The guard checked a small notepad, then let Jax and Joe through the gate into the fortress.

They arrived at the guardhouse at six o'clock. Inside, in a medium-size office, two men were waiting for them.

Joe recognized one as a fireman, even though he wasn't wearing his uniform. He was the same man who had walked through the Medieval Palace with Jax and Joe after the fire. The other man introduced himself as a Tower guard.

The two officials walked behind a large desk and sat down side by side. The guard gestured toward two chairs on the oppposite side of the desk. As Joe and Jax took their seats, the guard asked Joe the first question.

"And you are a friend of Mr. Brighton's?" he asked.

"I am," Joe answered. "I was here the night of the fire."

"Mr. Hardy was the one who found the knife," the fireman added.

"Ah, yes, the knife," the guard said, turning to Jax. "Did you bring it with you?" he asked.

"Here it is," Jax said, handing it over to the guard. He had wrapped the knife in a piece of canvas cloth.

"You said on the phone that this is not your knife," the guard said. "Is that correct?"

"Yes, it was my father's," Jax replied.

"I see," the guard mumbled. "And your father is—"

"He passed away two years ago," Jax said abruptly. "Why are you so interested in this knife?" he asked. "Is it because it was in the Palace? I believe Nick Rooney explained that I have been doing some work for the Tower. I created all the teeth—"

"Yes, yes, he told us all of that," the guard said, waving his hand in the air as if it didn't matter. "And you use the boning knife to cut the teeth somehow?"

Joe didn't like the way the guard asked the questions. He could tell that the man seemed suspicious of Jax. He looked at his old friend. Jax looked nervous. He was blinking his eyes and fiddling with the cloth that he'd wrapped around the knife.

"No, I don't use the boning knife on the teeth," Jax said. "I am also a taxidermist. I stuffed the two ravens in the Palace throne room, for example."

"He did a good job on those," the fireman said to the guard. "I noticed them right away."

"I'm sure he did," the guard said, never looking away from Jax. "But I'm simply trying to understand why he had this knife last night. As I understand it from Mr. Rooney, you were installing the finished heads on the wax bodies. Is that correct?"

"Yes, but—"

"And how did the boning knife fit into that task?" the guard asked, picking up the knife.

"It didn't, but—"

"So you were not using the knife for the heads," the guard interrupted. "And how about the ravens? Were you stuffing them last night? In the Palace?"

"No, of course not," Jax said. "They had already been done. The knife—"

"So you had no real reason to have the knife there that night?" the guard asked, putting the knife back down on his desk. He glared at Jax, frowning. It was very still in the room as the two men stared at each other. Jax made no move to speak, and the tension between the two seemed to thicken the air.

"Excuse me," Joe finally said to the guard. "If you'll just let Mr. Brighton answer your questions, I'm sure he'll be able to clear up any confusion," he said.

The guard leaned back in his chair. "I will be addressing you in a moment," he said. "Very well, Mr. Brighton. Enlighten me."

Jax took a deep breath. "The knife is just one of many implements that I use for my craft," he said. "I have several different bags and kits full of tools. The knife must have been in the one that I brought that night."

Joe remembered that Jax had said he never took his father's tools out of the shop. He waited to see what his friend would say next. But Jax stopped there and just smiled at the guard. It looked as if he was forcing himself to be friendly to his interrogator.

"'Must have been?'" the guard repeated. "Are you saying that you aren't sure yourself how the knife got there?"

"Well, no, not exactly. Of course it had to have come from my bag, I guess. It's definitely my father's knife."

"And when did you take it out while you were in the Palace?" the guard asked. "For what purpose were you handling it when you were there?"

Jax edged toward the front of his chair. "Look, exactly what are you getting at here?" he asked. His voice had taken on an irritated tone. "I've already told you I had no use for it there that night," he continued. "Perhaps it fell out when I got some other tool. Perhaps I took it out in order to reach something else and left it on a table by mistake. If you're saying that I took the knife so that I could cut a wire and start the fire, you're wrong. You're absolutely wrong."

"You're a dentist by trade, I believe." A different voice filled the room. Joe, Jax, and the guard shifted their attention to the fireman.

"An orthodontist," Jax corrected him.

"Yes," the fireman acknowledged. "We found this substance near the source of the fire," he continued, opening up a package of wax paper. Inside was a wad of something that looked like plastic.

"That looks like dental compound," Jax said. "As

you've been told, I formed all the teeth for the wax figures. I used that compound for part of the process."

"There's nothing suspicious at all about finding that in the Palace," Joe pointed out. "Jax had been there several times, fitting the teeth and working with the figures."

"Yes, I suppose you're right," the guard said, turning toward Joe. "Tell me, Mr. Hardy, just what were you doing there that night?"

"My brother, Frank, and I are old friends of Mr. Brighton," Joe answered. "We were invited to come with him that night."

"And when did you discover the knife?" the guard asked.

"After the fire, while my brother and Mr. Rooney met with the fire chief and Tower guards, Mr. Brighton and I surveyed the fire scene. This gentleman monitored us the entire time." Joe nodded toward the fireman.

"While we were walking around, I spotted the knife. I didn't pick it up until I was cleared to do so. It obviously belonged to Jax, and the guard allowed him to take it. It was not suspicious because Jax had been in the Palace several times with his tools."

"Yes, well, if you don't mind, Mr. Brighton, we'd like to hold this knife here for a day or two while our investigation continues. I will be happy to give you a receipt." The guard wrote a note on a piece of paper and handed it to Jax. Then he stood up, indicating that the interview was over. Everyone else stood up too.

"Thank you for coming in," the guard said. "We will be contacting you." He walked around behind the desk, and Jax and Joe headed for the door.

"Mr. Hardy," the guard called out as Joe stepped onto the cement stoop outside the door. Joe turned and looked at the guard. "How long have you known Mr. Brighton?" the guard asked. His lips spread out in a thin smile.

"He is an old friend," Joe replied. "In fact, he came to America and stayed with my family while he was studying there. You may have heard of my father, Fenton Hardy. He is a colleague of yours, in criminal justice."

"How interesting," the guard said. "I shall be sure to check him out."

The door closed behind Joe and Jax. There was no light except for a bit coming from a crescent moon and from the few security lamps on the Tower grounds.

Joe checked his watch. "I wonder what happened to Frank," he said. He reached for his cell phone and dialed the familiar number.

"Hey, bro, what's up?" he asked when Frank answered the phone.

"I was just going to call you," Frank whispered. "I'm in this church, St. Martin-in-the-Fields—down in the crypt."

Joe knew there was no point in asking his brother to speak up. If Frank was whispering, there was probably a good reason.

"So are you still with the mysterious woman?" Joe asked.

"Yeah, but I'm not sure why anymore," Frank said, his voice still low. "She's doing some art project in this small area down here. I've been watching her since we got here, and there's nothing weird going on. I'm walking right now to an area where I can talk better."

"He says he's in a church called St. Martin's something," Joe said to Jax while he waited for his brother to relocate. "The woman's doing some sort of art project."

"St. Martin-in-the-Fields," Jax said. "The London Brass Rubbing Centre is there, down in the crypt. They're famous for having a great collection of brass castings and moldings. They also supply colors and paper. People go in and make rubbings of these castings that they can take home, frame, and hang on their wall."

"What do you mean, 'brass rubbing'?" Joe asked.

"You place a paper over the casting, then rub it with a chalk crayon. The design from the casting appears on the paper."

"Oh, right—I know what you mean," Joe said. "We use that technique sometimes in detective work. You can use it with ID tags or coins or tombstones—anything on which the words or numbers are hard to read. You put a piece of paper over the object and rub a pencil over the paper, and the information just appears."

"Exactly," Jax said.

"Are you still there?" Frank asked in Joe's ear. This time Frank's voice was accompanied by a low hum of chatter and an occasional ringing noise, as if glasses were being clinked together.

"Where are you?" Joe asked. "I thought you said you were in a crypt. It sounds more like a restaurant."

"There's a café down here too," Frank said. "They're setting it up for some kind of party or something. I'm still walking down a hall, and now through some arches." Another pause. "Okay, it's quieter here. I can talk without someone hearing me. How's the interview going in the Tower?"

"It's over. And I gotta tell you, they were kind of rough on Jax. They treated him as if he were somehow responsible for the fire or something."

"Who are you? Why are you here?" Joe heard a strange man's voice with a heavy accent filtering through the earpiece of his phone. His heartbeat seemed to stop for a second. Through the phone he could hear Frank and another man talking.

"Hey, man, take it easy," Joe heard Frank say. "I'm just talking on the phone here."

"No—you are causing trouble," Joe heard the strange voice mutter. "But not any more."

"Frank!" Joe yelled into the phone. His voice seemed to echo around the massive empty Tower of London fortress. "Frank! What's happening?"

"Mmmgmfph . . . crckkkk . . . uumph . . ." The sounds that Joe heard were not good—and they could mean only one thing. Frank was in trouble.

7 The Eyes Have It

"Joe! You're white as a ghost!" Jax said. "What is it? Who's on the line?"

"Frank!" Joe yelled again into his phone. But he heard nothing. He stayed on the line just in case and sprinted to the gate of the Tower of London with the cell phone next to his ear. "Come on!" he yelled back to Jax. "Frank's in trouble!"

Joe and Jax left the Tower and raced across the street to the Underground. They jumped on the train and streaked through the tunnels of the Tube to the Charing Cross station. While Joe listened to his phone, calling to Frank in an effort to reconnect, Jax called the security number for St. Martin's. As they rode through the city, they caught pockets of phone reception.

They emerged from the Underground at the world-famous Trafalgar Square. The National Gallery of Art was across one street. Forming another side of the square was St. Martin-in-the-Fields.

Jax led Joe into the side entrance of the St. Martin's crypt. Occupying the basement of the church, the crypt had been a burial ground centuries ago. Now it had become a tourist attraction with a gift shop and café. But the remnants of the crypt were still evident. Embedded in the floor were tombstones labeled with the names of the bodies buried below the feet of visitors to St. Martin's.

Joe darted ahead when he heard his brother's voice. He and Jax wound through the arches in the crypt until they found Frank talking to three men.

"Hey," Frank said. He flashed a smile at Joe and Jax. "Did you call for this posse?"

"It sounded like you needed some help," Joe said. "Jax called these guys before we got into the Tube. I knew they'd get here faster than we could."

Frank let the medic check over his arm, but Joe could tell that his brother was feeling restless. "I'm fine," Frank said. "I need to—"

"Sir, you don't look fine," the man said. The man's name tag identified him as an employee of St. Martin's. The other two wore white jackets with the name of a London hospital printed on the back.

"Just have a seat, sir," the man with the medical bag said. "Let me take a look at your arm."

"Can you tell us how you got this injury?" the St. Martin's employee asked.

"Um, I work in the café," Frank answered. "I'm new. I was taking a break and bumped into someone coming around the corner. The collision sent me into the edge of the archway and I jammed my shoulder."

"So it was an accident?" the medic asked.

"That's right."

"Well, you seem okay, except for that shoulder," the medic concluded, closing up his bag. "Looks like you might have injured your rotator cuff. You'll probably want to have that X-rayed, just in case. Take it easy for a while—no lifting with that arm. Don't swing it around, especially up or back. It might take some time for it to heal completely."

"Actually, I've had a rotator cuff problem before," Frank said. "Injured it in a soccer match. So I know what to watch for."

"Very well, then," the St. Martin's man said. "I guess we are no longer needed." With smiles and nods all around, he and the other two medics left.

Joe waited until he could no longer hear their footsteps in the hallway. Then he turned to his brother. "How are you really?" he asked Frank.

"I'm fine, *really*," Frank said, getting up from his seat. He made a few tentative passes through the air with his arm. When he'd gone too far, he felt a familiar twinge of pain. "If it feels like I need more tests, I'll go in for them," he added. "But I'm okay for now."

"So what happened?" Jax asked, following Frank into the hall.

"I'll tell you in a minute," Frank said. He led Jax and Joe past the café tables and on to the Brass Rubbing Centre. As he'd expected, the mysterious woman was gone.

"We lost her—*and* the guy," Frank said.

"You mean the woman you followed here, right?" Jax said.

Frank nodded.

"But who's the guy you're talking about?" Joe asked.

"When you called me," Frank said, "I was watching the woman in the Brass Rubbing Centre. I walked back into the hall where I could be alone to talk, but some man followed me. He asked who I was and what I was doing here."

"I heard that on the phone," Joe said.

"Right. Well, I told him I was just talking on the phone," Frank continued. "But he didn't believe me. He grabbed my arm and twisted it behind my back. He wouldn't tell me who he was, of course. And he said he knew I'd been following someone and had to stop—that if I didn't, I'd pay. He gave my arm a final twist, and then dropped it and started to run away. When I grabbed his jacket, he wriggled free. I started after him, but the medics stopped me."

"The woman is the key, don't you think?" Joe guessed.

"Yes," Frank said. "And she looks familiar."

"I know," Joe said. "Let's work on figuring that out—we're bound to place her if we really rack our brains."

"Maybe some fuel will help," Frank said. "I'm suddenly starving."

"Hey, I still need some dinner too," Jax said. "That Tower interrogation left me weak. Now I know how the royals must have felt before their beheadings on the Tower Green. How about some food? There's a place near my flat that I can't wait to show you."

Jax, Frank, and Joe grabbed the Tube. While they rode, Frank told them about the man who'd attacked him.

"Obviously a friend of the woman who was following us," Joe concluded.

"Yeah. I wish I could remember why she looks so familiar," Frank murmured.

They got off the train in Jax's neighborhood. At eight o'clock they rounded a corner onto a street of small houses. A black sign dangled out from the building on the corner. Painted on the sign were plain white words: BLACK BELT.

"There it is," Jax said.

"No way," Joe said. "Karate?"

"Remember the fun we had taking lessons when I was staying with you guys?" Jax said, clapping Joe on the back. "You're really going to like this place."

The club was full of young men and women sitting

at tables and in booths. In the far corner was a small stage.

"This place has karate exhibitions and amateur competitions at nine," Jax pointed out. "If you want to, you can even participate. You just sign up, and you can either do a single demonstration or pair up with someone else."

Jax took a flyer from the stack on the stage. "How about it?" he asked. "Shall we show them what we learned? Check it out." He handed the flyer to Joe.

Jax's cell phone rang while the Hardys read the rules for the amateur karate exhibition. Jax talked for a few minutes, then hung up.

"It was Nick," he told the Hardys. "He's on his way. I'm going to run to the flat and pick up a raven for him."

"Stuffed, right?" Joe said, grinning.

"Indeed," Jax confirmed. "It's an extra one for the exhibition. Nick will be surprised when he sees it. I told him I wouldn't get it done in time."

"I'm coming with you," Frank said. "I want to get some heat on this shoulder. I brought some sports salve that'll do the job."

"Hold our table," Jax said. "We'll probably be back before Nick gets here."

"I'll even save a chair for the raven," Joe said.

When Frank and Jax got to the flat, Jax went into his taxidermy shop and Frank went upstairs. His shoulder was really aching, so he headed right for the guest bedroom. He got the tube of medicine from his sports bag and rubbed the cream into his shoulder.

A rush of heat flooded his aching rotator cuff and radiated around his shoulder and up the side of his neck. For a second it felt like his skin was on fire. Then the feeling settled into a comfortable and soothing warmth. He tried a few flexes and was pleased that his arm was loosening up.

He pulled on a fresh shirt and headed back down to the taxidermy shop.

Just walking in the back door of the shop was an eerie experience. The only light came from a few tiny bulbs glowing in a couple of display cases, and from the streetlight beams through the shop windows.

Hairy hides hung from hooks, a drawer of glass eyes stared up at him, and noses and ears poked out of cotton batting. Shadows of animal parts played across the walls like a freaky sci-fi film.

Frank couldn't tell which felt stronger: the radiating heat in his shoulder or the cold chills everywhere else.

He heard a rustling noise in the front room of the shop, and then a click. "Jax?" he called out, walking toward the front.

The moment he stepped into the room, the cold chills won out. Jax lay on the floor, a huge blue-black raven across his chest. Neither was moving.

8 The Cavity

"Jax!" Frank yelled. "Jax—say something!"

Frank smacked the stuffed raven away. It flew off Jax's chest and slid on its back across the wood floor.

An involuntary shudder rippled down Frank's spine as he reached for Jax's pulse. His own heart was beating so fast that he couldn't feel his friend's at first. Finally he felt the rhythm of Jax's heartbeat. It was faint, but it was there. Frank knew he didn't need to use CPR.

He looked closely at his friend's face. Jax's eyes were closed, and his mouth was slightly open. There was a pink mark on his right temple.

Frank went to the shop phone and dialed the emergency number that was stuck to the receiver.

71

It was like dialing 911 in America. He gave the dispatcher the address of the flat and told her Jax's condition. Then he hung up and called Officer Somerset.

The policeman was not in, but Frank left a message saying there had been a forced break-in at the taxidermy shop, Jax had been injured and taken to the hospital, and Frank didn't know what had happened.

He went back to his friend, who was lying on the floor. The large welt on Jax's temple had billowed up from the skin's surface and was now a darker red. "Jax!" he called again. "Can you hear me? Wake up, man."

Ideas and images flooded his mind. He noticed an old-fashioned blackboard on the wall. On it, someone—probably Jax—had drawn a diagram of a fish with white chalk.

Frank took the chalk from the ledge and drew marks around Jax's body on the floor. He made the marks very faint so that they wouldn't attract the attention of the ambulance crew that was on its way.

Beads of sweat broke out on Frank's face as he drew the outline. "This is just for the record," he mumbled to himself. "For *our* investigation. Jax is alive—and he's staying alive."

At last he heard the welcome two-tone siren of the ambulance. The vehicle skidded to a stop in the lane outside the shop. Two emergency medical technicians jumped out. One grabbed a medical bag from the back of the ambulance. The other carried in a gurney.

Frank rushed to unlock the door. It opened easily, and he realized that the antique lock had been broken.

While the EMTs assessed Jax's vital signs, one of them asked Frank what had happened. He told them honestly that he didn't know. He showed them the jimmied lock and explained that there had been recent burglaries in the area.

"We're going to report this call to the police," she said.

"I've already done that," Frank assured her. "You can check with Officer Somerset."

It took only a few minutes for the EMTs to check Jax and get him loaded onto a gurney. Then they flipped the spring that dropped the wheeled legs of the bed. They were so preoccupied with their job that they didn't notice the pale chalk line left on the floor when they raised Jax's bed.

The EMTs rolled the gurney out of the shop. Frank followed closely behind. Jax was still unconscious. The medics told Frank the address of the hospital and pushed the gurney into the ambulance. Then they sped off with lights blazing and siren whooping.

Frank raced back into the shop and turned on all

the lights. Then he carefully examined the floor where Jax had been lying. Little by little, he spread out his search to include the path from the door, and compared it to the location of Jax's body.

He felt the creepy sensation of dozens of eyes watching him as he moved among the stuffed creatures that inhabited the shop. As in the storage room above, the eyes seemed to follow him as he searched.

The lighting in the store wasn't good, and the floor was distorted by weird shadows. "Probably helps sales to have it dim and spooky in here," Frank whispered. He took out his penlight and aimed the beam at the floor around the chalked image of his friend.

He widened the circle farther and farther until he reached the door with its broken lock. But he found nothing—no clue to the person who had broken in and attacked Jax.

Frank wasn't willing to give up yet. Beads of sweat crept down his back. He was determined to find out what happened to Jax.

He'd learned from countless previous investigations that a second search can often solve the case, so he decided to reverse his search. This time he would begin at the door and move back to the chalk line.

He moved the penlight beam into the dark corners around the door and the adjacent display cases. This time he moved the light slowly, inch by inch. And this time he saw something. A sudden sparkle like a micro-firework shot up into the penlight beam as it passed by—then it disappeared. Frank edged the light back, and there it was again. A shimmer.

Frank grabbed a chamois cloth from the top of one of the display cases. Then he crouched down and reached for whatever was glittering, shielding his fingerprints with the chamois.

What he found was a small round plastic case. It was about half the size of the container that holds a roll of film.

He opened his hand to look more closely at the object that was nestled in the cloth. Inside the clear plastic case was a powder that looked like sand but emitted the rainbow colors of a crystal prism in the light.

He moved the penlight beam back and forth across the case. The powder changed colors like a hologram. The bottom of the case was stamped with an odd symbol. It looked like a V.

Frank wrapped up the case and dropped it in his pocket. Then he turned off the shop lights and closed the front door. Because he could no longer lock it, he pushed a heavy display case against the door.

Except for the case of powder in his pocket and the chalk outline on the floor, he tried to leave the room exactly as he'd found it. Finally, before he left, he took one last look around and then exited the same way he had come in: through the back door of the taxidermy shop.

He didn't look forward to his next move. As he walked up the staircase to the second floor, he thought of his brief conversation with the EMTs about the break-in.

What if the person who broke in tonight wasn't just your run-of-the-mill local burglar? Frank thought. He felt the sudden thump of his pulse pumping through his neck. *What if he wasn't just looking for preserved animals and birds—or even money? Maybe he was looking for something with much more value. . . .*

He went into the kitchen. On a hook in the pantry were spare keys to all the locks on both floors of Jax's property. He had showed them to the Hardys when they first arrived. Frank grabbed the key to the medical suite.

He hurried out of the living quarters and into the suite. He walked through the reception area and the treatment rooms. Everything looked okay. Then he got to the lab, and his stomach knotted into a ball. Someone had gone through everything in a hurry. There wasn't a lot of damage; the instruments and machines seemed untouched. But drawers were hanging open and had been emptied. Cupboard doors were ajar, and what had been on shelves was now on the floor.

Frank walked into Jax's office. More of the same. "Whoever went through these rooms was not out to cause damage," Frank whispered, "and wasn't just looking for something expensive to steal. This thief was after something specific."

Frank crossed to the file cabinet. It was near the wall, but not as close to the wall as Jax usually kept it. He slid the file cabinet farther from the wall, as Jax had done when he'd showed them his secret hiding place for the Molar Mike. "There's the heating grate," Frank whispered. He crouched down and pulled the grate open. Behind the grate was the safe door.

His hands felt clammy. He rubbed his palms against his jeans.

Frank punched into the keybad the sequence of numbers Jax had shown them. With a barely audible click, the safe door opened slightly.

He crooked his finger around the edge of the door and pulled. "Just as I'd thought," he whispered, staring at the black emptiness inside. "Nothing."

9 Ground Under the Underground

Frank shut the door to the empty safe, closed the grate over the safe door, and pushed the file cabinet back against the wall. The safe was completely hidden again.

He quickly checked the rest of the office. Then he went into the lab and looked around there. He was careful not to move anything in case the police might need to gather fingerprints later. He found nothing out of place since the last time he'd been there, just after the press conference.

Frank felt a sudden urgency to get to Joe and tell him what had happened. Quickly he closed up the medical suite and left the flat. He raced up the lane and around the corner to the Black Belt.

"Hey, there you are," Joe said, as Frank hurried

up to the table. "I'd decided it was time to come get you guys. What took you so long? Where's Jax?"

"Probably in X-ray," Frank said in a low voice. He dropped into a chair and told Joe what had happened.

Joe stood up so quickly that he knocked his chair over backward. He plopped a few Euro dollars on the table to pay for his lemon drink. "Let's go," he said. He pulled out an Underground map and plotted out the route they'd use to get to the hospital.

"There's more," Frank said, just after they stepped outside. He pulled Joe to a stop. "The Molar Mike is gone. The safe was empty."

"Empty?" Joe repeated.

"The tooth, the test results—everything is gone," Frank said.

"Someone broke in to steal the Molar Mike, and Jax must have surprised him," Joe concluded. "So the thief knocked him out."

"Sounds right to me," Frank said. "But we can't be sure until we talk to Jax."

"What do you mean?" Joe asked.

"The safe was locked, and the file cabinet was in place," Frank reminded his brother. "It looked like everything else was secure. Maybe Jax moved the tooth to another secure place and just didn't have a chance to tell us."

"So we don't call the police on this yet?" Joe finally concluded.

"I called Officer Somerset from the flat to report the break-in and Jax's accident," Frank said. "But since there's an outside chance Jax moved the tooth himself, I didn't mention the empty safe. We can't know what happened there for sure until Jax is conscious again."

Outside the Black Belt, the air was gray and wet. Frank realized he had been so preoccupied with what had happened at the flat that he hadn't even noticed the fog until now.

They could see only a few feet in front of them. People walking toward them seemed to suddenly materialize, as if they'd been silently squeezed out of the soupy mist.

"Turn around, guys—you're going the wrong way. The Black Belt's behind you." They heard Nick's familiar voice ahead of them before they actually saw him. And then, *bam!* There he was, a yard away.

"Jax has been hurt," Joe said, forcing his words through the fog. "We're on our way to the hospital now."

"Whoa—I'll go with you," Nick said, quickly reversing direction and falling into step with the Hardys. "What happened?" he asked as they took the steps to the Underground two and three at a time.

"We don't know," Frank said. He decided to respect Jax's privacy and not to say any more until he talked to his old friend. Frank knew that Joe would pick up on his strategy.

The three of them were quiet on the ride to their first connection. While they stood waiting for the second train, Joe finally spoke. "Jax says you were speaking to some school group tonight?"

"Sort of," Nick said. "It's a private group that works with underprivileged youth. I talked about the history of the Tower. They seemed to like it. How about you two? How'd you spend your day? How did Jax's press conference go?"

"Pretty straightforward, until the end," Frank said. "You'll read about it in the papers tomorrow, I'm sure." He told Nick about Geoffrey Halstead's appearance.

"What a mess that must have caused," Nick said. "That's a real blow."

"I went with Jax to the interview with the Tower guard," Joe said. "He and the fireman really grilled Jax. They acted like he was a suspect."

"Oh, I don't think so, really," Nick said. "I've talked to them about Jax, told them he's first rate. I'll check in with the guard tomorrow—see if I can pick up anything from him. And I'll make sure he understands that Jax should not be considered a suspect."

When they got to the hospital, the doctor talked to them. They were all relieved to hear that Jax had a mild concussion, but no broken bones or permanent damage. He was still unconscious, but his vital signs were good. The doctors were monitoring him closely to make sure he did not slip into a coma.

"Do you need to have your shoulder looked at while we're here?" Joe asked his brother.

"Nah," Frank said. He knew that it was a good idea, though, so he ultimately gave in. His self-prescription was confirmed: heat, rest, no lifting, no moving his arm back and up.

After Frank was released, he, Joe, and Nick went back out into the fog. It was even more dense and wet than before. And Frank noticed that something new had been added: an icy current of air that wove in and out of the mist. It seemed to go through his clothes, and even his skin and chill him from the inside out.

"Man, this weather is the worst," Joe said with a shiver. "It doesn't matter what time of year it is. The fog always makes it feel like winter."

"I know just the thing to warm us up," Nick said. "It's just a few miles from here. The Tube will get us there in no time," he added. He squinted his eyes. A few pale colors glowed in the thick clouds. "There's the station," he announced.

Nick led the Hardys underground again. But this time, when they got off the train they realized that this was one of those stations that was completely above ground. The fog was a little thinner here. They could see across the tracks into the windows of the apartment building on the other side.

Within minutes, they were in a small restaurant called the Fire Pit. It was not quite ten o'clock.

Tables and chairs surrounded the crackling fire in the center of the room. Curls of heat wrapped around the diners and helped them forget the gloomy air outdoors.

"Fish and chips is it for this place," Nick told the Hardys. "I insist that you get it. If you don't like it, I'll eat it for you."

They placed their orders and drank hot coffee while they waited.

"So, Jax will be all right, don't you think?" Nick asked.

"That's what the doctor said," Joe said.

"And what about you?" Nick asked Frank. "What *is* a rotator cuff, anyway, and how do you hurt it?"

"It's a band of four muscles that are strung together," Frank said, forming a circle with his hands. "They make a ring around the shoulder joint and give it support. It actually looks like a cuff made out of muscles."

"How did you injure it?"

"I fell," Frank answered, without missing a beat. "I fell hard on my shoulder and kind of twisted it."

"Was this when you tumbled down the stairs last night?" Nick asked.

"Yeah," Frank lied. "That's when it happened." He just didn't want to share any of the evening's earlier events with anyone until he'd talked to Jax.

"Have you figured out who did it yet?" Nick asked. "Jax told me you two are detectives. Do you know who broke into Jax's flat and tossed you down the stairs?"

"No, not yet," Frank said.

"Jax said you caught Pierre Castenet sneaking around later," Nick said. "That guy's a real nutcase."

"He's pretty weird all right," Joe agreed. "And he really wants to get his hands on the Molar Mike."

"Well, I hope you don't have it on you, because he's heading our way," Nick said.

Frank and Joe followed Nick's gaze and saw Pierre storming toward them. He was wearing the same red-and-white workout suit he'd been wearing the last time they saw him.

He stopped at their table and bumped Joe's chair. "Okay, what's going on?" he said in a loud voice. Several people at nearby tables looked over with startled expressions.

"Hey, Pierre, what's happening?" Joe said. He sat on the edge of his chair, ready to spring. Pierre seemed to be in the mood for a fight.

"That's *my* question," Pierre snarled. "Are you two following me?"

"We're just here for some fish and chips," Frank said. "Why? Should we be following you? Have you done something we don't know about yet?"

"Absolutely not!" Pierre bellowed. Out of the

corner of his eye, Frank saw one of the waiters and another man coming over.

"I already told you everything," Pierre said. "And I told Scotland Yard too. And thanks to you, my hotel room was searched and my passport was lifted. I told them I didn't see anybody else around Brighton's flat. But apparently they don't believe me. So I'm warning you just this once. Stay off my back, or you and Jax Brighton are going to be very sorry!"

"Excuse me, gentlemen," the man with the waiter said. "I'm the manager of this restaurant. Will you please take this discussion outside? You're disturbing the rest of my customers."

"I don't need to take anything outside," Pierre said, still staring at Joe. "It's settled. Leave me alone . . . starting *now*." Pierre spun around and stomped out of the Fire Pit.

The manager scuttled after him, and the nearby diners went back to their meals.

"Well now, this place *is* fun, isn't it?" Nick said, grinning at the Hardys.

Frank and Joe looked at each other. They each knew what the other was thinking: *He's warned us—stay on guard.* Frank nodded his head and then looked around the room. "It seems Mr. Castenet got a little too close to the fire pit."

"You know, this building is ancient," Nick said. "It's been a public gathering place of one form or another since Henry VIII."

A waitress brought a tray heaped with large cones of newspaper. Each cone was lined with wax paper, and it cradled huge chunks of fried fish. Nestled around the fish were dozens of equally huge chunks of potatoes—crispy brown on the outside, soft and mashed on the inside.

All three of them agreed it was just what they needed. They sprinkled malt vinegar down into the cone and dove into their hearty meal.

"Speaking of the ancient royals," Nick said, "the exhibit is still on for Sunday. The Palace won't be cleaned up by then, but they moved the exhibit to the Waterloo Block. That's the same building where they exhibit the crown jewels. I hope Jax gets back on his feet soon. I need his help."

"We're checking in on him again in the morning," Frank said. "If he's awake, we're going over first thing."

By the time they finished eating it was ten thirty, and Nick announced he had to get home. They all went across the street to the above-ground Underground station. Nick went toward the tracks for the eastbound train, and the Hardys went to the tracks for the westbound.

The fog was very dark and dense. Joe could feel it creeping into his eyes and through his teeth. It had a musty, sooty taste.

Visibility was so bad that he could only hear the

trains rattling into the station. He couldn't see them until the engines plunged the trains through the fog curtain a few yards away.

Joe looked around and realized that he and Frank were the only ones left on their side of the tracks.

A chill rippled along Joe's arms, and he wished he'd worn a warmer jacket. "I'd forgotten how the weather is in London. The air is so cold and wet," he said.

He looked to his left, where Frank had been standing, but he saw nothing but the greenish-gray cloud-fuzz of fog.

"Frank? Hey, where did you go?" A nervous chuckle seemed to stick in his throat.

He heard a shuffling noise on his left, and then a couple of footsteps.

"There you are," Joe said. "I was beginning to think . . . *Mmwhoomph!*"

He felt two hands wham into his side, forcing the end of his sentence out with a gush of air. For an instant he couldn't breathe.

Finally he was able to manage a huge gulp of wet air. All he could think about was grabbing the person who'd given him the side chop. He started to turn, but it was too late. He felt another blow jamming into his side again.

A wave of pain flooded through Joe's body. The ground suddenly seemed to fall away under his feet as he sailed off the platform. A black object flew out into the emptiness with him. He fell onto the cold subway tracks, and a black shoe landed a few feet away. He felt the tracks vibrating beneath him. With an ear-splitting whine, the train barreled through the tunnel opening . . . and then through the fog . . . moving directly toward him.

10 Trapped in the Web

"Joe! Joe, where are you?" Frank called across the tracks.

Joe shook his head. It was like the fog had seeped inside his brain. It seemed to take forever for him to become aware again. First he felt the subway tracks under him. Then he heard Frank in the distance, calling his name. But Frank's voice was quickly drowned out by the rumbling of the train coming toward him.

At once all his senses surged. He knew he didn't even have time to stand up. With a powerful lunge, he rolled once, twice, and one final time.

The force of the passing car blew him farther away from the tracks. Joe sighed with relief as the train ground to a stop.

"Joe!" Frank yelled from the other side of the train car—the side where Joe had stood before being forced out onto the track.

"Joe, answer me!" Frank called.

"I'm okay," Joe said, pulling himself up. He did a quick mental check and realized he really *was* okay. Nothing broken, nothing sprained.

"I'm out on the tracks," Joe called back. "But I'm on the other side of the train."

Just then an Underground security officer showed up and began yelling to Joe to get off the track.

"Excellent idea," Joe said. "I'm on my way. But first I have to find something." He looked back to the spot where the shoe had landed, but there was nothing there.

The security man scolded Joe when he got back to the platform. He obviously didn't believe Joe's story and thought Joe had jumped onto the tracks for the thrill of it. He told Joe, with a grimace, to stay off the tracks, and left.

"I couldn't figure out what had happened to you," Frank said. "Someone brushed by me and knocked me onto a bench. By the time I got back over to where you'd been standing, you were gone."

"The word 'gone' is a little too close to the truth for me," Joe said. And whoever it was didn't just brush into me. I was pushed—or maybe kicked— onto the tracks."

"Kicked?" Frank repeated.

"The first blow felt like a karate chop, and the second was like a kick," Joe said. "And by someone who really knew what he was doing. But whoever it was lost a shoe doing it."

Joe rubbed his side as he told Frank about the black shoe that traveled through the air with him. "It's gone," he said, looking around. "Wait a minute!" he cried. "Look!"

Joe pointed to the familiar yellow train car he had seen Wednesday night. "It's the tunnel cleaning train!" he said. "Remember? I told you about it."

Joe ran back across the tracks, with Frank following close behind. Joe talked the tunnel cleaning driver into letting him look at the last few things the car had sucked in. Fortunately the driver could release the last few gallons of trash without having to open the whole carload.

With a wheezing belch the first item dropped from the car. It was a black shoe, now slimy from the tons of garbage and trash in the car. Frank grabbed a newspaper left on a bench, wrapped it around the shoe, and handed it to his brother. Joe tucked it under his arm, and the Hardys caught the next train bound for Jax's neighborhood.

At midnight Frank and Joe climbed the same stairway they had barreled down the night before. This time, though, there were no surprises waiting for them at the top.

As soon as they got to their room, Frank showed

Joe the case of shimmering powder that he had found on the taxidermy shop floor.

"That stuff looks like the inside of a shell," Joe said. "Like those abalone shells we found on the beach in California."

"And it might not even be a clue about the identity of the thief," Frank pointed out. "Jax might use it in his taxidermy stuff. We can check with him tomorrow if he wakes up."

"So do you still think it's possible that Jax was attacked by the burglar who's been hanging around this neighborhood? And that it has nothing to do with the missing tooth because Jax moved it himself to a safer place?"

"I'm just saying it's possible," Frank said. "And I'm not going to blow Jax's cover if that's what happened."

"Okay, I can see that. But what if that's not the case?" Joe persisted. "If someone has stolen the Molar Mike . . ."

Joe let his thought trail off as he got out his notebook computer. He opened the lid and fired up the machine. Then he continued his thought.

"Okay, I'm thinking we're going to find out that Jax did not move the tooth," he told Frank. "And if he didn't, we can bag the idea that some stranger broke in."

"Meaning, it wouldn't be that thief who's been hitting around here lately—the burglar that Officer Somerset told us about," Frank said.

"Exactly," Joe continued. "You said everything else in the place is the way it was when we last saw it."

"Right," Frank agreed.

"So if someone stole that tooth," Joe said, "it has to be someone who knew the layout of this place. Someone who knew right where to go to find the safe and the Molar Mike. Someone who didn't need to tear the place apart to find it."

"Like Pierre Castenet," Frank said. "Don't forget that he was prowling around the medical clinic last night before he ran to the top floor to hide. And he sure was threatening us at the Fire Pit. Maybe he had more of a reason to run than he admitted."

"And we already know he's been bugging Jax for the tooth," Joe added, typing "Pierre Castenet" in the search box on his screen. "Let's just see what the Internet has to say about him."

"Was the person who brushed by you at the station wearing red and white, by any chance? Maybe he kicked me onto the tracks."

"It happened so fast, and besides, I couldn't see anything in the fog. I'm going to check on Jax," Frank said. He dialed the hospital and asked for the nurse's station on Jax's floor.

While Frank made his call, Joe searched for information about Pierre Castenet. They each finished their task at about the same time.

"Good news," Frank told his brother. "Jax is still unconscious, but not in a coma. The doctors think he should be awake in a couple of hours. They're ordering no visitors until tomorrow, but it looks like we'll be able to talk to him in the morning."

"Great," Joe said. "That means we can find out more about the tooth. Then we'll know our next step." Joe saved some Internet data about Pierre Castenet into his documents file. "I've got some news too. Take a look at this."

Frank bent over Joe's shoulder and read the three screens as Joe clicked through them.

"Hmmmmmm . . . Looks like Pierre's gotten into some trouble back home," Frank noted.

"He's got the reputation of being the kind of coach who'll do anything to win," Joe said.

"That just might mean he'd be the kind of coach who'd steal the Molar Mike, take it back to Canada, and smuggle it through customs—"

"And stick it in his team captain's mouth—" Joe continued.

"To send illegal plays to his team," Frank finished.

Joe switched screens. "Check this out," he said. "He's already had a lot of legal problems. There have been a couple of fights and lawsuits from the victims. Plus he's had some major fines imposed on him by this semi-pro league his team plays in. Then last year he got into a big jam—he was charged with embezzling money from the players' pension fund."

"How'd he manage that?" Frank asked.

Joe clicked to the final screen. "He's got partial

ownership of the team. It's not a big stake, but it's enough to have access to the pension fund. It seems he took advantage of that and ripped them off."

"What I want to know is how he's managed to stay out of jail," Frank said. He straightened up and perched on the edge of the table. His shoulder ached, so he rubbed the muscles in his upper arm.

"Until recently he bought himself out of trouble," Joe told his brother. "Now that they've found out where he got the money, it's a whole new ballgame. Plus he's in a lot more trouble now because his team isn't winning anymore. There's been a lot of commotion among the press and the public demanding that he be fired."

"Of course, he might be able to fix that losing streak if he has a hidden receiver and mike planted in one of his key players," Frank suggested.

"Exactly," Joe said.

"I still don't understand why he's not in jail."

"Apparently he's worked out some payment plan that will reimburse the fund," Joe said.

"And if he loses his job, he won't be able to keep up the payments," Frank observed. He rubbed some more of the medicinal cream into his shoulder.

"How's your shoulder?" Joe asked.

"Better," Frank said. He made a few small circles in the air with his arm. "It really is. How's your side?"

"Sore. Pass some of that salve over, okay? Have you remembered anything more about the guy who twisted your arm?" Joe asked, rubbing the cream on his bruised side. "Anything at all?"

"Nothing," Frank said. "I've been over the scene in my mind a hundred times. It's like the guy who knocked me down the stairs. I've got absolutely nothing on either one."

Frank began pacing as he talked. "I saw the guy in St. Martin's running away, but it could have been anybody. Stocky guy, bomber jacket, stocking cap."

"He accused you of following someone, so he's got to mean that woman," Joe said.

"Who was actually following *us*," Frank added.

"I only saw her from a distance," Joe said, "but like I said earlier, I know I've seen her face somewhere before."

"Definitely," Frank said. "I saw her through the binoculars, and I agree with you. She looks like a woman Dad chased down a few years ago, right? I don't remember the case. Let's dig into Dad's files and see if we can find her."

Frank and Joe's dad, Fenton Hardy, was a professional detective. He was known by criminal justice authorities all over the world for his work on international cases.

Joe called up a special Web site, and then entered the set of passwords necessary to access their father's case files. His father had entrusted these passwords to his sons. In return, though, they'd agreed to use them discreetly.

"Go right to the international cases," Frank said. Joe pulled up the list. Many of the listings included a photo of the culprit involved.

They spent the next half an hour scrolling down the list, checking photos, and reading case summaries. Occasionally they found a photo that seemed promising, but when they read about the case, they found out the woman had died or was in prison.

"Man, he's been busy!" Joe commented as he continued to scroll down the list. "Way to go, Dad!"

"Hold it," Frank said. "Stop right there." The tone of his voice made Joe lift his fingers right off the keyboard.

"Enlarge that face," Frank ordered.

Joe put the mouse cursor on the photo and clicked. The image expanded to fill the screen.

"There she is," Frank said. "That's the woman."

11 Message from Mike

Joe looked at the computer screen. Frank was right. The woman glaring back at them was definitely the woman he'd seen through the binocular lenses the evening before.

"Hmmm, no name," Joe murmured. "The only ID the authorities have on her is 'AA42.' That's pretty weird."

"Looks like she was a spy for the former Soviet Union," Frank said, scanning the screen, "but they don't have any country affiliation listed since the U.S.S.R. broke up."

"Could be that she's a freelancer now," Joe offered.

"Ever since we first heard about the Molar Mike," Frank said, "I've thought the perfect application for it would be espionage. How great would it be to be in constant contact with a spy who is working for you? And best of all, the person wouldn't be wearing an obvious microphone that the enemy could find."

"You're right," Joe agreed. "Constant contact with agents in the field would be ideal. Especially if the enemy didn't know that the spy was wired to headquarters."

"It says she did some of her best work as a spy in London," Frank said. "But it says here that after her cover was blown, she got out of the business."

"Or did she?" Joe wondered. "Getting her hands on the Molar Mike would guarantee a great comeback."

"If the Molar Mike *has* been stolen," Frank said, "she moves to the top of my suspect list."

The Hardys climbed into their beds just after midnight. Frank's shoulder ached and now burned from a new application of the medicated salve. Joe's mind just wouldn't turn off.

"We definitely have to check on that shoe," Joe said as he turned over.

"Mmhmmm," Frank murmured in agreement as he shifted his focus from his shoulder to Joe's voice. "Tomorrow," Frank mumbled.

By the next morning the gloomy weather had broken, and thin shafts of sunlight streamed through surprisingly white clouds. The Hardys were standing up in Jax's small kitchen, eating scrambled eggs and spicy sausage straight from the skillet.

"Hurry up," Joe said, swallowing his last bite. He washed it down with a tumbler of orange juice. "I can't wait to see how Jax is doing."

"Let's hope he's put the Molar Mike someplace besides the office—somewhere safe," Frank added. He grabbed the chamois cloth with the small container of shiny colored powder and dropped it into his pocket along with the photo of the pewter fragment. Joe shoved the cleaned-up black shoe in his backpack. Then they locked up the flat and left.

When the Hardys got to the hospital, they found Jax sitting up in a chair by the window, eating a big breakfast.

"I saw you guys walking up to the entrance," he said. "I hope you're here to spring me from this prison."

"Show a little gratitude," Frank said with a grin. "They did a good job on you. You were a pretty pitiful sight when you came in here."

"Okay, I'll grant you that," Jax said, pushing away his tray table. "Now get me out of here."

"First we have to tell you something," Frank said, pulling a chair over to the window where Jax was sitting. Joe eased himself up to perch on the edge of the bed.

"You look kind of serious," Jax said. His forehead crinkled into a frown. "What's up?"

"Do you know why you're here?" Frank asked.

"What do you remember about last night?"

"Not much," Jax said. "I had gotten the raven for Nick in the taxidermy workroom. I heard a noise in the shop in front and went to see what it was. I don't really remember anything else. But I gather it was some sort of foul play."

"That's right," Frank said. "We think someone knocked you out."

"Officer Somerset was here about an hour ago," Jax said. "He thinks it was some sort of burglary or attempted burglary. The front door was jimmied open, so I called this morning and asked a local handyman to board it up. We won't know what's missing until I get out of here and check. So it was probably that guy who's been breaking in around the neighborhood, don't you think? The person who'd broken into the flat the night before?"

"Maybe," Joe said. "You didn't see anyone before you got hit? Or hear anything besides that one noise?"

"That's right," Jax said.

"How about smells?" Joe asked. "Did you smell anything odd?"

"That's a funny question for a taxidermist," Jax answered. "There are so many odd smells in my lab." He stopped to think, then finally answered, "But, no, I can't recall smelling anything. What's going on, you two? I get the feeling there's something you're not telling me."

Frank told Jax how he had found him in the shop.

"And there's more," Joe said. He looked at Frank and nodded.

"After the paramedics took you out of the shop, I looked around," Frank continued.

"Did you find anything?" Jax asked, leaning forward in his chair.

"I did," Frank said. "But I'll get to that in a minute. The main thing is what I *didn't* find."

Jax looked as if he were trying to figure out what Frank meant. Then his eyes popped wide open, as if he'd just seen a ghost.

"You're not telling me . . ." Jax began, but his words trailed off as he looked over at Joe. Joe just nodded his head.

Jax looked back at Frank. This time his eyes narrowed into little dark slits. "Did you check the safe?" he asked in a very low voice. "Did you?" he repeated. "Was it there?"

"The safe was empty," Frank said.

Jax slumped back into his chair. He rubbed his forehead with his fingers, as if he were trying to erase Frank's words from his mind.

Joe hopped off the bed and came over to stand by Frank's chair. "We were hoping it might be somewhere else," Joe said. "Everything was in place in your office, and the safe door was closed. So we thought there was a chance you had moved it."

"No, I didn't," Jax said. He sat up again, alert, his shoulders tensed and stiff-looking.

"You have copies of all the specs and plans, I'm sure," Frank said.

"Of course," Jax said. "I even have another prototype of the transmitter itself. It's not in a tooth, but it could be. But whether I have other copies isn't the point."

"We know," Joe agreed. "If one of them hits the black market, the value of your invention drops through the floor."

"It becomes practically worthless," Jax said. "But there's more to it than that. It's my creation. My patent gives me exclusive production for at least a decade, so I can regulate the quality—and that's really important to me."

Frank related his steps leading up to finding the empty safe. "We haven't reported the theft yet," he added. "We wanted to talk to you first, to make sure it was really stolen."

"You said there was something you were going to tell me later," Jax said, "about something you found?"

Frank took from his pocket the container of powder he'd found not far from Jax's unconscious body. "Is this yours?" he asked. He handed Jax the container, using the cloth so as not to mess up any fingerprints.

Using the cloth the same way Frank had, Jax held the container under the lamp.

"This is pearl essence," he said. "I have some in my shop. It's finely ground mother of pearl, derived from shells. I use it sometimes in my taxidermy mounts, to create the iridescent effect of fish scales. They shimmer and look absolutely like the real thing. But this isn't mine," he added. "I've never used any containers like this. I don't know what this symbol is." He pointed to a small icon on the canister.

"Do you want to call Officer Somerset and tell him about the Molar Mike?" Joe said.

"No!" Jax said. "I don't want the police on this yet."

"Are you sure?" Frank asked.

"What if it was taken for ransom?" Jax suggested.

"You mean some kind of toothnapping?" Joe asked.

"Why not?" Jax said. "I just announced the Molar Mike yesterday. And last night, it's stolen. If someone contacts me for ransom, I'm going to pay it. Only *I* know how valuable that invention could be. I'll pay anything to get it back."

"You really don't want to let this trail get any colder," Frank warned.

"I've already got the two best detectives I know working on the case for me." Jax gave the Hardys a small smile as he spoke. "You guys see what you can find out. Give it a few days before we call in the police—at least until I'm released. I'm hoping that will be tomorrow or the next day. If it was stolen for ransom, we should have some word by then from the thief."

A burst of noises at the door caught everyone's attention. Three people walked in at once: a doctor, Nick, and a nurse partially hidden by a huge bouquet of flowers.

Jax greeted them. "Just the people I've been waiting to see," he said with a slight smile. "Nurse, tell the doctor how well I am. Doctor, sign me out of here. Nick, drive me home."

"Hey, Jax. Am I glad to see you among the living," Nick said, clapping Jax on the shoulder. "I need you back to work."

The nurse put the large vase of colorful blooms on the bedside table. Smiling, she came over to take Jax's blood pressure while the doctor read his medical chart. The Hardys and Nick stepped out into the hall while Jax was being examined.

From the hall Frank watched the nurse finish up and roll the blood pressure cuff back up. Then the doctor took over, checking Jax's eyes and reflexes.

Frank walked to the drinking fountain at the end of the hall while Joe and Nick talked. From the corner of his eye he saw the nurse pass by. She stopped a few feet in front of him, then turned back.

"Would you do me a favor?" she asked him. "This card was in the flowers that I brought up for Mr. Brighton. I forgot to put it back when I left the vase." She reached in her pocket and took out a small envelope.

"I'll give it to him," Frank assured her.

The nurse walked on down the hall, and Frank turned back to the water fountain. As he sipped, he replayed in his mind the conversation he, Joe, and Jax had shared before they were interrupted. *Toothnapping . . . ransom note*, Frank thought. *Could Jax be right?*

He wiped his hand across his dripping mouth and stepped into the shadows at the end of the hall. He pulled the flap from the unsealed envelope the nurse had given him. Inside was a plain white card with a message hand printed on it:

Hey Dad—miss me?
Get 100,000 euros together.
I'll tell you later where to bring them.
Then I'll come home.

M. Mike

12 The Fog of Fear

Frank took a big breath—he realized he hadn't taken one since before he read the ransom note—and then he hurried to Jax's room. Joe and Nick were back inside.

"The new wax figures have been poured," Nick was saying, "and I've got a crew working on the costumes and accessories at this very moment. We have lots of extras in storage. We salvaged a lot of the teeth from the fire wreckage. I need you to clean them up and repair what needs fixing, and get them into the heads as soon as possible."

Nick turned to the physician. "What do you say, doctor? When can I take my friend home and chain him to his worktable?"

"I believe we can release him this afternoon," the

doctor said. "I'm waiting for the results of the test we took this morning, but I'm expecting it to be favorable. I'll check back with you in a couple of hours, Mr. Brighton."

"Excellent," Jax said.

The minute the doctor left the room, Jax began talking. "I didn't think they'd ever leave," he said. "We've got to talk more about the tooth."

"What tooth?" Nick asked. "The Molar Mike? What about it?"

"I want to tell Nick what happened," Jax told the Hardys. "This guy's got a network that won't quit. He's worked all over the world and has contacts everywhere."

Quickly Jax told Nick about the theft of the Molar Mike.

"What did the police say?" Nick asked. "Do they have any leads?"

"I'm not telling them yet," Jax said. "I think the tooth has been taken for ransom. And if the thief thinks the police are in on this, I'll never see the Molar Mike again."

"What about that guy who's been bugging you to let him try out the tooth?" asked Nick. "That coach from Canada. He seems like a pretty good bet to me." He told Jax about their encounter with Pierre at the Fire Pit.

"And he did case your flat two nights ago," Joe added.

"I think you're making a mistake by not calling the police," Nick said. "You don't even know for sure that you're going to get a ransom note."

"He does now," Frank said, taking the envelope from his pocket. "The nurse said this came with the flowers."

"I was wondering who sent them," Jax said. He took out the card and read the note out loud.

"Whew, a hundred thousand euros," Nick said. "That's a lot of change."

"The Hardys are super detectives," Jax told Nick. "I'm counting on them to help me find the tooth before it gets on the black market. With their detecting skills and your international network, we're bound to solve this case."

"Okay, I'm going to get right on it and see what my buddies around the world have heard," Nick said. "In exchange, you get out of this place and help me get the exhibit ready for Sunday."

Nick bolted out of the room with an encouraging wave.

"So the exhibit is on anyway?" Joe asked.

"Yes," Jax answered with a grin.

"Do the Tower guards know you're still working on the exhibit?" Joe asked. "I mean, they seem to think you're an arson suspect."

"You're going to love this," Jax said with a gleeful grin. "They not only checked out your dad, as you suggested, but they were so impressed with who he is, they actually *called* him. Apparently he vouched for my sterling character."

"Thank you, Dad," Joe said, smiling. Then he told Jax about being kicked onto the Underground tracks.

"Whoa . . . hold on!" Jax jumped to his feet, then reached for the chair to steady himself. "This is getting way too serious. I don't have any right to put you in this kind of danger."

"Hey, I'm okay," Joe assured his friend. "The sooner we get this guy, the safer we'll all be."

"Do you have any suspects, Jax?" Frank asked.

Jax shook his head and suddenly looked downcast. "What am I going to do, guys? I don't have a hundred thousand euros. Everything I have is tied up in the tooth."

"Who do you think stole the tooth?" Frank asked again.

"You can start with Geoffrey Halstead," Jax said.

"The jeweler?" Frank said, surprised. "He's already suing you for stealing the idea from him. He doesn't need to steal the actual tooth."

"Yes, he does," Jax reasoned. "He doesn't have a case for his lawsuit, I can guarantee that. And I've heard rumors around the neighborhood shops that his business is in financial trouble."

"Maybe that's the real reason behind his suit," Joe offered. "He's not in it for fame or recognition for being the inventor. He needs money to save his business."

"Except it will take years just to work his lawsuit through the system," Jax pointed out. "And he's got to know I will never settle out of court with him voluntarily."

"So you're saying he stole the tooth. But why?" Frank asked.

"To force me to make a deal with him," Jax answered. "He holds the Molar Mike for ransom. I get the tooth back, he drops the suit, and he gets money to cure his financial ills."

"In other words," Joe said, "you think he's jumping over the courts and going straight for the money? Holding the prototype for ransom so he can settle out of court?"

"Exactly," Jax said.

"Okay, he definitely has pretty easy access to your place," Frank said, his mind gearing up to full speed. "His jewelry store is right there. Nobody's going to think it's odd if he's hanging around the area."

"Speaking of jewelry, what about that pewter piece Frank found?" Joe said. "Maybe it's something he was working on or repairing for someone."

"And the pearl essence you found, Frank," Jax said. "He might use that in one of his jewelry creations."

"He could have been the one we surprised that first night," Joe said. "I didn't get a good look at the face of the guy who threw you down the stairs, but the body type and size would fit Halstead's."

"Okay, we'll check him out," Frank said.

"And Nick's right—we can't rule out Pierre, either," Joe said. He told Jax what he'd found out about the coach's legal and financial problems.

"Well, the top of my list belongs to AA42," Frank said.

"What's an AA42?" Jax asked.

"Not a *what*," Joe answered, "but a *who*."

The Hardys told Jax everything they knew about AA42.

"I always knew the Molar Mike would be a valuable weapon for investigation and for information gathering," Jax said.

"She knows where you live because she followed us yesterday," Frank pointed out. "She's also a top spy, with all the experience, skills, and tools she needs to pull off the theft."

Frank stood up. "Okay, we've got to get to work. You pay attention to the doctor and call us if you're released."

The Hardys left Jax's room at noon. Once outside the hospital they stopped at a food cart and picked up some sandwiches and sodas. They walked to a small park and sat on a bench to eat their lunch—and between bites, they planned their strategy.

"I'm going to try to see Pierre," Joe said. "I'll go back to the flat where Jax thinks he might be staying. I want to see if he's been straight with us or not. I'll also check out a few stores and see if I can

112

find out anything about this shoe. I've never seen one like it before."

"I'm going to start with Geoffrey Halstead," Frank said, "and then I'll try to track down AA42. The only place we know she might be is St. Martin's. Maybe the attendant at the Brass Rubbing Centre knows something."

"Let's keep in touch," Joe said, checking his watch. "It's about twelve thirty now."

The Hardys finished eating, and Frank went to the Underground to catch the train back to Jax's neighborhood. The sun was still shining as he walked the few blocks to Geoffrey Halstead's store. The front door of Jax's taxidermy shop was boarded up, just as Jax had ordered.

Frank walked into the jewelry store next door. There was no one there. "Mr. Halstead?" he called out. No one answered. "Mr. Halstead? Anyone here?"

Still no answer. Frank made a few loud noises, but there was no response. He walked to the back of the store and peered into what looked like a workshop. "Mr. Halstead?" he called. When there was no answer again, he stepped inside the room.

Beautiful, polished tools nestled in flannel cloths sat on a long table. Magnifying glasses were perched on top of flexible arms on heavy stands. Small vises and saws were bolted to the edge of the table. No jewels or precious metals were visible, but there were several large black cases in the back of the room, and each of them had a digital combination lock. Frank suspected the jewels were inside.

A couple of shelves lined one wall. As Frank stepped over to get a closer look, he had an odd feeling: Someone was watching him, he was sure of it. He whirled around just in time to see a tall, thin man with dirty blond hair standing right in front of him. His arm was raised—and in his hand was a thick wooden pole.

13 Tracking Suspects

The stranger swung his arm down, aiming the pole at Frank's head. Frank raised his own arm and blocked the man's blow, then punched the man in the midriff with all the strength he could muster. The adrenaline was racing through his system so powerfully that he barely felt the pinch of his rotator cuff.

"Unnnghhh!" the man groaned as he doubled over, and the pole clattered to the floor. Frank pumped his knee up into his attacker's chin, and the man crashed onto his back. He looked up at Frank with a dazed expression, and then his head fell back almost in slow motion. He was out.

Frank scrambled around the workshop until he found a long, heavy chain and a padlock. He wrapped the chain around the man's wrists and ankles and secured it with the padlock. The he ran his hands over the man's pockets and carefully pulled out a revolver. He placed the weapon on top of a display case and called the police.

Checking again to make sure his prisoner was still unconscious, Frank checked the rest of the store. He found Geoffrey Halstead in the bathroom bound with rope. A cloth was tied around his mouth.

As soon as Frank released him, Geoffrey took a deep breath. "Thank you, thank you," he said.

Frank showed Geoffrey the man on the floor. "That's him," Geoffrey said. "That's the man who tried to rob me. He has a gun somewhere."

"It's up there," Frank said, pointing to the weapon. "What happened?"

"I was working on a necklace behind the counter, and he snuck up behind me," Geoffrey said, running to his case in the front of the store. "Several pieces are missing. He must have them on him somewhere."

"We'll wait for the police," Frank said. "I've already called them. There—I hear the sirens now."

Two police vehicles rolled up. A couple of officers jumped out of a van. Officer Somerset and a policewoman were in the car that followed.

The policewoman talked to Geoffrey about what had happened. Frank led Officer Somerset and the other two officers over to his prisoner.

One of the officers checked the prisoner's pulse. "Sleeping like a baby," he reported.

While Frank told Officer Somerset what had happened, the other two policemen began frisking the man. His pockets were full.

"My necklaces, my brooches," Geoffrey wailed, as the officers laid out the jewelry.

"Mr. Halstead seems to be fine physically," the policewoman reported. "He's pretty shaken by the experience, though. I was able to get a full statement from him. We should finally be able to put this guy away for a while."

"Well, it looks as if you might have caught our neighborhood burglar, Mr. Hardy," Officer Somerset said. "He fits the description of the thief we've been seeking. He has the stolen items on his person. And it sounds as if Mr. Halstead can give us an eyewitness account of an actual burglary. I have to agree with my colleague. This case seems closed."

"What case?" a familiar voice called from the front door. "What's going on?"

"Jax!" Frank called. "You're out of the hospital."

"Indeed," Jax said. "I took a cab home but was surprised to find police cars in front of my flat. What happened?"

"This time it was your neighbor—Geoffrey Halstead—who had an encounter with the burglar," Officer Somerset related. "But due to the excellent skills of your houseguest, we seem to have the culprit in custody."

"Great, Frank," Jax said, clapping Frank on the back.

The other two officers escorted the chained prisoner out to the van. The man had awakened by now and was mumbling something about being innocent.

"Mr. Hardy, the city of London thanks you, as do I," Officer Somerset said. "We may have to call on you for more information or further identification, but I assure you, we will not bother you needlessly. If this goes as I expect, we will wrap up this case for good in a short time—and you and your neighbors will recover your stolen items, Mr. Brighton."

"I'm afraid I have something more to report," Jax said. "It's kind of a long story. But I will not tell you unless I can count on your absolute confidence."

Officer Somerset sent his three colleagues off with the prisoner in the van. Then he, Frank, and Jax stepped outside the store to talk in private.

"You might not have heard of this yet, but I invented a device called the Molar Mike," Jax said.

"I read about it just today," Officer Somerset related. "It is fortunate that it was not stolen by the person who broke into your store yesterday."

"As a matter of fact," Jax began, "it was."

Frank and Jax told the officer about the theft, explaining why Jax had not reported it yet. "Now

118

that it looks as if Frank has caught our local burglar, it seems a good idea to tell you. Please keep your eye out for it when you search the burglar's belongings and residence."

"Do you have the ransom note with you?" Officer Somerset asked.

"I do," Jax answered, reaching into his pocket. "You understand that we have to keep this from getting out, because if it does, I may never see my invention again."

"Excuse me, but can we get a copy of that before we turn it over?" Frank asked. "There's a copier in the back of the store."

"I don't see why not," Officer Somerset replied.

Frank went to the back of the jewelry store. Geoffrey's attention was completely absorbed by taking inventory of the stolen items. He barely responded when Frank told him he was going to use the copier.

Frank put the copy of the ransom note in his pocket and brought the original back to Officer Somerset.

"I'll assume you will not be getting any more notes because I believe the writer is now in our custody," the policeman said. "But if you should receive more, you must let me know immediately."

"Yes, I will," Jax said.

"Now I'd better take a look at your office and lab," the policeman said.

"You two go ahead," Frank said. "I want to ask Mr. Halstead a couple of questions—as a customer."

Jax and Officer Somerset walked around the store toward the staircase that led up to Jax's flat. Frank walked back into the jewelry store.

"Mr. Halstead," Frank began.

"Please call me Geoffrey, and I shall call you Frank. After all, you saved my life and my store."

"Great," Frank said. "I just have a couple of questions to ask you—and they have nothing to do with what happened today. Think of me more as a customer."

"I'm at your service," Geoffrey said, smiling.

"I'm looking for a pewter clasp," Frank said. He took out the photograph of the fragment he'd found and showed it to the jeweler. "As you can see, this one is broken and I'd like to replace it. It's sort of a leaf shape and has a hinge on one end."

"I see that," Geoffrey said. "I've never had anything like that, but I specialize in custom-made jewelry. If you left this photograph with me, I'm sure I could make a satisfactory replica for you."

"Thank you," Frank said. "I'll definitely consider that. Now I have another question." He closed his fingers around the small container of pearl essence in his pocket.

"I have a string of clear glass beads that I bought for my girlfriend back home," Frank said, weaving the story as he went along. "I haven't given them to her yet because she recently told me she really wants some pearls. I figure maybe a jeweler like you can fix up these beads I bought to make them look like pearls?"

"I don't follow you," Geoffrey said.

"I mean, maybe you have some paint or some kind of material that you can put on these beads so they'll look like pearls?"

"Surely you're joking," Geoffrey said. "I would never, *never* try to pass glass off as pearls. You can buy ready-made imitations at any ordinary store. You don't need to engage a master jeweler to create them for you."

"Okay. Well, thanks," Frank said.

Frank walked up the stairs to Jax's flat and went immediately to the office in the medical suite. Jax and Officer Somerset were there, looking over the damage. Then they all went down to the taxidermy shop and checked it. They found nothing new.

"Try to get us an inventory of everything that's missing as soon as possible," Officer Somerset said. "That may help us build our case against the man we now have in custody. And thank you again, Mr. Hardy, for your fine work."

Jax let the policeman out the back door of the shop, and then he and Frank went upstairs to the flat.

"I brought in the mail," Frank said. "It's on the kitchen table."

Jax flipped through it, but found nothing interesting. "I'm going to shower," Jax said. "I want to get the hospital smell off of me."

"Okay, I'm going to check in with Joe." Frank went to the small sitting room at the front of the flat. The red light on the phone answering machine was blinking. "Jax, you have some messages," he called to his friend.

Jax walked in and punched the button. There were three calls. The first was from Nick, hoping Jax was back home and ready to go to work on the exhibit. The second was from Fenton asking his sons to call him. The third was from someone who sounded as if he was disguising his voice.

"Hi, Dad," the voice said. "It's me, Molar Mike. Put the money in a locked black briefcase and bring it to Signer's Wharf tonight at midnight. Leave it behind the newspaper stand. Then I can come home."

14 The Chill of
Discovery

"Play the message again," Frank said.

Jax pushed the play button on his answering machine. The voice asking for the ransom was not the only sound on the tape.

"Can you turn up the volume?" Frank asked.

Jax booted it up to the highest level. Frank could hear someone else speaking.

"Do you hear that?" Frank asked. "It sounds like a show going on in the background, someone talking steadily. And there are other noises too. People talking and laughing. Be sure to make a copy for us."

"Sure," Jax said, "but I'm not turning this over to Officer Somerset."

"Jax—," Frank began.

"I know, I know," Jax interrupted. "It's the smart

thing to do. It's also a sure way to lose control of my invention for good." He looked at Joe with a determined glare. "I can't take that chance," he added. "This is my call, Frank. I'm making it."

Frank knew his friend well enough to know how stubborn he could be. He decided to drop the subject for now and bring it up again when Joe could make it two against one.

"Okay," Frank said.

While Jax was in the shower, Frank played the ransom tape again and again, as loud as he could. But he couldn't make out the words in the background.

Next Frank returned his dad's call. "So you fellows are pretty busy over there, I take it," Fenton Hardy said.

"Our usual vacation," Frank said with a chuckle. "Can't seem to get away from the family business, Dad."

"I'm sure you've heard that the Tower of London called me about Jax," Fenton said.

"Yes—and thanks for the support."

"No problem. There's no way Jax Brighton is going to be setting fires in the Medieval Palace— and I told them so. I also got an interesting e-mail from one of my buddies in Scotland Yard. He told me you caught some burglar who's been plaguing the city for weeks. Congratulations! I'm really proud of you."

"Thanks, Dad," Frank said. He always felt good when his father told him that.

"So what about Joe?" Fenton said. "It's his turn to catch a crook, right?"

"As a matter of fact, he's tracking one right now. Jax is in trouble, and he's asked us to help him out." Frank outlined the case and told his father about the suspects. When he mentioned AA42, his father interrupted him.

"I know the woman you're talking about," Fenton said. "And you'll probably have to drop her from the list of suspects."

"You're kidding! Why?"

"The latest word on her is that she's working both sides of the fence now."

"You mean she's a double agent?" Frank asked.

"Looks like it," Fenton confirmed. "I can't tell you for which countries, but apparently she's basically on our side—for the time being, at least. Best to leave her alone right now."

The two Hardys talked a little longer and finally hung up. Jax came in from the kitchen, gulping water from a bottle, just as Frank was about ready to call his brother.

"Do you know where Joe is right now?" Jax asked.

"Not a clue," Frank answered as he punched in the number of Joe's cell phone. "He was going to try to track down Pierre. He was also going to see what he could find out about that shoe that was kicked into the subway tracks."

"Hey, Frank, what's up?" Joe asked on the other end of the line. Frank told him about his call to their dad and the ransom call to Jax. Then he asked Joe how his afternoon had gone.

"Pitiful," Joe said. "First I headed back to that flat where Jax thinks Pierre might be staying. It was only about seven blocks from the park where you and I had lunch. I stopped in a couple of sporting goods stores on the way. No one had seen that black shoe before. One guy thought it might be custom-made, and he gave me the names of a couple of people who might make it. I was trying to call you—I take it you're not tracking AA42 after what Dad said?"

"Right," Frank agreed. "I'm at the flat. What about Pierre? Was he at his friend's place?"

"No, but I talked to a woman who lives there. She's the wife of his friend. She said he went home, back to Canada. But she acted kind of weird. She might be lying. I called Officer Somerset and left him a message about it."

"Ask Joe if he signed us up for karate tonight at Black Belt," Jax said. "I won't be able to make it, but Nick could fill in for me. He's a black belt too."

"Did you hear that?" Frank asked his brother.

"Yeah," Joe answered over the phone. "Tell him I didn't sign us up—I'll wait until he's back to full strength. Hey, I'm wondering about something. . . ."

Joe was quiet for a few seconds. Then he spoke again. "You know, Nick seems to be a pretty multi-talented guy. You know? He told us he'd been a TV news anchor, a foreign language translator, a historian, a craftsman, and a restorer. Doesn't he seem kind of young to have done all that?"

Frank turned to Jax. "How long have you known Nick?" he asked.

"Less than a year," Jax answered. "Actually he's been with the Tower longer than he usually stays with a job, according to him. He kind of follows his instincts about how long to stay in one place and when to cut and run."

"Did you hear that?" Frank asked Joe again.

"I did," Joe said. "Ask him who else knew about the Molar Mike before he announced it. Besides Geoffrey, Pierre, and Nick."

Frank asked Jax his brother's question. Then he held the phone out so Joe could hear Jax's answer.

"I have no idea," Jax said loudly, so Joe could hear him clearly. "As I said before, I don't really think Geoffrey knew because when we talked early on, I wasn't specific about the invention. We were just discussing microreceivers in general."

Jax sank into a chair and took a few deep breaths. Frank could tell he was still a little weak from his knockout the night before.

"What did the doctor say you were supposed to do when you got home?" Frank asked.

"He said I could do anything I felt like, but to take it easy. He thought I might be a little woozy. Looks like he was right."

Jax grabbed a couple of gulps from his water bottle, then continued to answer Frank's question. "When Geoffrey read about the press conference, he must have put two and two together."

"Who else knew?" Frank prompted.

"Well, Pierre learned about it from the manufacturer I hired in Canada. I have no idea how many leaks there were out there and who was able to pick up on them. That's why this whole thing is so frustrating."

"It's almost six o'clock. Come on back to the flat, Joe," Frank said. "We have to talk."

"Actually I just got on the Tube—we're above ground at the moment," Joe said. "I'll be there in a few minutes."

By the time Joe got to Jax's lane, the sun was too low behind the buildings of London to provide much warmth any more. The trees that hung over the street rustled as the evening fog and breeze began filtering through. The old-fashioned streetlights popped on, but their beam was muted to a pale glow.

Joe was the only one on the block. He could feel the black shoe bouncing around in his sports bag as he broke into an easy jog.

Jax's lane was narrow to begin with, but it was

made even more so by haphazard parking on both sides of the street.

He was just a few yards away from Jax's flat when he heard the *vroooom* of a small car tearing down the street toward him. With a sudden squeal of brakes, the car came to a quivering stop right next to where he stood.

The door opened and Pierre Castenet stepped out. He wore jeans and a bright red windbreaker, and his bulk seemed to fill the little street. He slammed the door so hard, the whole car rocked a couple of times.

"I warned you," he snarled.

15 Trailing a Rat

Pierre took a few steps closer. He outweighed Joe by at least fifty pounds, but Joe stood his ground.

"What's the problem, Pierre?" he asked, slowly dropping his sports bag on the sidewalk.

"The problem," Pierre hissed, "is you coming to my friend's house. The problem is you talking to my friend's wife. The problem is you and your brother not paying any attention to me when I tell you to leave me alone."

"Actually I'm surprised to see you," Joe said. "Your friend told me you'd gone back to Canada."

"Whether I stay or go should not be your concern," Pierre said, taking a few slow steps forward.

Joe didn't flinch. He stared into Pierre's eyes without blinking. "But it is," Joe said. "And as long as you keep bugging *my* friend, it will remain my concern."

Pierre's eyes narrowed. He seemed to be studying Joe, as if he were measuring up an opposing team. For a few seconds they stood a couple of yards apart. Neither gave an inch.

Finally Pierre blinked. He settled back on his heels and let out a sigh. "I don't need any more trouble," he said in a low voice. "Just keep out of my way."

He walked back to his car, climbed in, and peeled down the street.

Joe took a deep breath, picked up his bag, and walked around to the stairway that led up to Jax's flat.

"You missed my welcome party," Joe said. He told them about his standoff with Pierre.

"Sounds like you held him off," Jax said. "But I really don't think he's the one who took the Molar Mike."

"We don't either," Frank said, looking at his brother. Joe nodded.

"Jax, why don't you rest for a while," Frank said. "We're going to run a few errands. We'll even take the raven over to Nick for you."

"That would be great," Jax said, getting up to collect the stuffed blue-black bird.

Frank packed the pewter fragment, the container of pearl essence, and the copy of the ransom note into his backpack. Then he added a mini cassette player and the phone answering tape with the ransom message.

"Okay, we're out of here," Frank said to Jax. "Get some rest. We may have to put you to work later."

The Hardys jogged to the Underground station, and within minutes they were in the Tube—Frank, Joe, and the raven.

"Let's go back to our first night here," Frank said as they rode to the Tower of London. "Could Nick have been the guy that knocked me down the stairs?"

"Sure," Joe said. "I didn't see any red hair, but it could have been under that cap. And I didn't see his face at all. Remember, he didn't come back to the Palace with you after you two met with the fire chief and guard."

"Right," Frank said. "He told me he was going to stay late at the Tower and help with the clean-up and investigation."

"Then the guard who had interviewed Jax and me stopped us for another forty-five minutes so he could question you," Joe pointed out.

"Nick could have known we were being held up—or he could have even suggested that the guard talk to me. That would have given him plenty of time to get over to the flat and prowl around."

"And we know he was in the neighborhood last night when Jax was knocked out and the Molar

Mike was stolen," Frank said. "He popped up outside the Black Belt right afterward."

"He'd called Jax earlier, remember?" Joe said. "Jax told him we were all at the Black Belt. He probably figured he was clear to look around the flat. But he didn't know that Jax planned to surprise him by going back to pick up the raven."

"Plus, we were with him right before I was kicked into the tracks—"

"And he's got black-belt kicking legs," Frank concluded.

"I haven't figured out who's behind the fire in the Medieval Palace yet," Joe said. "But was it really an accident?"

"Hard to say," Frank guessed. "Jax is sure he didn't take his dad's knife over there. Nick could have lifted it from the taxidermy shop. Jax said that he's been there a lot since they've been working together on the exhibit. Maybe Nick was trying to set Jax up for some reason."

"That reminds me—remember when we all finished at the Palace and were going to Nick's flat for sandwiches?"

"Yeah," Frank said.

"He said he was going to check in with the guard, and he sent us on ahead. He could have planted the knife—"

"And the gasoline, and even the dental compound at that time."

"Exactly." Joe stood up as the train slowed down. "Here we are," he said. "Tower Hill Station."

Carrying the stuffed raven, Frank showed the guard at the gate the temporary pass that Jax had given him. Once inside, the Hardys walked straight to the employees' building. They walked up to the third floor and into Nick's quarters.

"Nick?" Frank called. "You in here?"

"He's over at the exhibit hall," a young woman answered from the corner of the messy room. She was working on a costume and was partially hidden by a large screen.

"That's in the Waterloo Block?" Joe asked.

"Yes," the girl said, not even looking up from her work.

"I guess you all are really busy now, trying to get all the new wax models ready for Sunday," Joe said. "Too bad there wasn't time to clean up the Medieval Palace." He continued to occupy the young woman's attention while Frank looked around the workshop.

It took Frank only a few minutes to find containers of pearl essence that matched the one he'd found in Jax's taxidermy shop the night the Molar Mike was stolen. He turned them over. They all had the same V on the bottom that his had. But the V was only part of the symbol. Each of the containers that were in Nick's quarters had a bird's head on the bottom, and the V formed the beak.

After a few more minutes the girl noticed Frank

poking around, so Joe quickly wound up their search by saying, "Well, I guess we'd better get the raven over to Nick."

Frank took his brother's cue, and the Hardys left Nick's quarters and walked over to the Waterloo Block. The building was temporarily closed to tourists while the new exhibit was being assembled. Frank flashed the pass at the guard, and they walked right in.

Visitors were guided along from room to room through the long building in roped-off aisles. Permanent exhibits explained the history of the Tower of London and the royal families who lived there.

The last room on the path held glass cases in which the collection of crown jewels was displayed. Elaborate crowns, jewelry, and other ornaments laden with diamonds, rubies, and emeralds sparkled under the special lighting. Scattered around the room, and roped off by velvet cords, sat the new wax models of kings and queens from British history.

"Frank, Joe!" Nick's voice echoed through the large room. "Who's your friend?" He smiled at the raven under Frank's arm.

"Jax finished it," Joe said. "That's what he was going to the shop to get last night when he was surprised by the thief and knocked out."

"Wow. He told me it wouldn't be done by Sunday. He's amazing. It's gorgeous, isn't it? It'll be perfect over here by the little fence in the corner."

Nick led them to a small scene he had created. The principal model was a male figure dressed in royal Scottish regalia.

"How's Jax doing?" Nick asked. "I'm hoping he'll feel like helping out tomorrow. I have an assistant who can probably fit the teeth, but it would be better to have the master himself here to do the job."

"The doctor said he could do anything he feels like doing," Joe answered, watching Nick closely. "He'll probably be okay by tomorrow."

"Just put the raven down by that man's boot, will you, Frank?" Nick requested as he fluffed up a clump of artificial heather. "I'm glad Jax is feeling okay," he added, without looking away from his task. "I'll give him a call in the morning and see how he's feeling."

Frank leaned over to drop the raven on the other side of the velvet cord. The wax model had on a richly colored plaid kilt, and a tassel hung from the belt.

As he leaned back up from the exhibit, taking a closer look at the belt, Frank stopped cold. Connecting the tassel cord to the belt of the kilt was a familiar object: a pewter clasp in the shape of a leaf.

136

16 The Beheading

Joe watched Nick closely, trying to get some clue—a gesture, an expression—anything that would indicate that Nick was a thief capable of assaulting someone he pretended was his friend.

Distracted for a moment, Joe looked at his brother. Frank was leaning over the velvet cord, studying something. He seemed almost frozen to the spot and looked a lot like the wax models placed around the room.

Joe followed Frank's gaze and saw what had rooted him to the model's belt—the pewter clasp.

Frank finally stood all the way up. "Well, our job is done here," he said, smiling at Nick. "Sorry we can't stay and help, but we've got other errands to run."

"Thanks for the raven, guys," Nick said. "Tell Jax I'll call him in the morning."

The Hardys walked back through the long building. Halfway to the entrance, Frank heard a familiar rhythm. "That's it!" he said. "Listen!"

"What? All I hear is some background noise. It sounds like chanting or a folksong—some singing group."

"Exactly," Frank said, pointing to the speakers in the ceiling. "It must be background music to provide atmosphere when tourists go through this part of the exhibits. But it's also the sound in the background of the ransom phone message!"

The Hardys left the Waterloo Block and began the trek across the grounds to the main gate.

"Man, that guy is so smooth," Joe said. "He acts like nothing's going on—like he's totally innocent of everything."

"We already know he's got contacts all over the world," Frank added. "We have to get him before he puts Jax's invention out on the black market."

"You're sure he's the thief?"

"Well, he's got the pearl dust in the exact same container as the one I found," Frank said. "I'd have guessed they came from the Tower earlier, if part of the icon hadn't been worn off the bottom of the one I found. The V is the beak of a bird."

"The Tower of London raven," Joe guessed. "Of

course. He probably uses that stuff to make fake pearl jewelry and decorations."

"That's what I figure," Frank agreed. "And now I can place that pewter leaf clasp. Jax says Nick is really strict about making the costumes authentic. The clasp is obviously an important part of that Scottish outfit."

"I'll bet when we check the custom shoemakers on that list, we'll find one who made a special pair of black cross-training shoes for Nick," Joe said. "Do you suppose he's really going to be at Signer's Wharf tonight for the ransom money? Or is that just a hoax so that everyone will think it's a toothnapping?"

"I don't know," Frank said. "But we'll be ready if he does show up." They boarded the Tube and began devising a plan.

It was eight o'clock when they got back to Jax's flat. They found him in the kitchen, eating a big bowl of stew. He looked a lot better and seemed to be glad to see the Hardys.

"Where have you guys been?" Jax asked, ladling stew into bowls for them.

Quickly Frank and Joe told their friend their theory about Nick, and the evidence they had found. Jax didn't seem as shocked as they had expected. "Nick's a weird guy," Jax told them. "This all makes sense. I don't know why I didn't see it myself."

"Do you feel like doing a little work?" Frank asked Jax after they'd finished eating.

"If it means getting the Molar Mike back, you bet I do."

"Good," Frank said. "Get that big, hairy brown rat I saw in the taxidermy shop, and let's get started."

They spent the next three hours wiring the rat with a microreceiver like the one in the Molar Mike. Then they wrote a computer program to transmit to it. Finally they were ready. Jax packed his notebook computer and the rat into a large duffle bag. Then he put newspapers in a black leather briefcase and locked it.

At eleven fifteen the Hardys and Jax took the Underground up to the canals and got off near Signer's Wharf. The fog was thick and heavy. They could barely see a yard in front of their feet. There was no sound other than the hushed lapping of the water in the canal against the piers, and the eerie sounds of restless animals in the nearby London Zoo.

Frank had insisted the three of them rehearse every move so they wouldn't have to talk when they reached their destination. When they arrived at the wharf, they each went to work.

Frank placed the briefcase exactly where the telephoned ransom message had demanded, behind the newspaper stand. He placed the rat close to the briefcase, and readily visible in the pale glow of an old light attached to the newsstand.

As he moved along the bank to some large

bushes, he heard little feet scampering away, and then small splashes as things plopped into the canal. He guessed that the sounds came from living relatives of the stuffed beast he had just placed nearby. Quietly he crouched behind the bushes among the scampering creatures.

Joe helped Jax position himself in the shadow of a tree—although, the fog was so thick that no one near the newsstand could possibly see him anyway. Then Joe moved to a spot where he could see the newsstand and Jax and Frank could see him.

They waited. As the minutes ticked away Frank could hear the creatures leaving the water and returning to join him. He steeled himself against the image that kept flashing through his mind: huge river rats sidling toward his feet.

Finally he heard larger feet nearing the area. *Definitely human,* he thought. Through a tiny space between the twigs and leaves of the bush that shielded him, he saw a man walking toward the newsstand. At first he couldn't see any of the man's features. Then, as the man leaned over to pick up the briefcase, Frank caught the swing of a dark red ponytail.

Frank looked at Joe, and they nodded at each other. Joe waited until the man's hand was nearly on the briefcase handle, and then he signaled Jax.

"Hey Nick, how's it going?" The question vibrated through the fog.

141

Nick jumped back and seemed to notice the rat standing nearby.

"Yeah, it's me." The voice definitely came from the rat. Nick couldn't take his eyes off of it.

"You've already got the tooth," the rat said. "Seems a little greedy to stick him for the money, too."

Nick stepped back another foot and whirled around. His face showed that he suddenly understood completely what was happening. He looked like he was choosing between fight or flight.

Flight.

Frank and Joe each popped up from their concealed vantage points and took off after Nick. Joe tackled him, and Frank wrestled Nick's arms together, behind him. Nick fought like any good black belt would, but it was too late. The Hardys already had him down. Frank handcuffed him—wrists and ankles—with antique cuffs that had belonged to Jax's dad.

"You're a real piece of work, Nick," Jax said, joining them.

Nick's expression of defeat disappeared, and he grinned proudly. He struggled to sit up, and rested his arms on his bended knees. "Yeah, I am, aren't I?"

"Where's the Molar Mike?" Jax demanded.

"You will never know, my friend," Nick said, still grinning. "I'll take it to my grave before I'll tell you."

Jax lunged for Nick, but Joe pulled him back. "Did you call the police?" Joe asked Jax.

"Yes," Jax answered. "As soon as he began to run—like the rat he is."

"You might as well give it up," Joe told Nick. "The police will frisk you when they get here."

"And they won't find a thing," Nick told them. "I never intended to give it back. The ransom money was going to help finance my getaway. Plus, I figured if I asked for a ransom, I'd scare you off from contacting the police, Jax."

"Did you set the fire?" Frank asked.

"Yep. And it was such a pleasure. I didn't want that stupid exhibit anyway. I tried to tell everyone that, but they overruled me. I planned it perfectly."

"But why set up Jax?" Joe asked. "Why plant the knife and the other stuff? What did that get you?"

"That was an added stroke of genius on my part," Nick answered. "I figured planting a little suspicion of Jax might just get him out of the way. Then I'd have room to get my hands on the Molar Mike. I'm going to set up a worldwide auction for that juicy little tooth. The highest bidder gets it, and I don't care who it is."

"You were the one who knocked me down the stairs that night, weren't you?" Frank asked.

"Indeed. You surprised me by being home so early. I thought the Tower guards would keep you engaged much longer."

"And you knocked me out last night when you

stole the tooth and all the materials that go with it," Jax said.

"Right," Nick said, nodding. "I'm always prepared to seize an opportunity. I enjoy being spontaneous. When Jax told me you were all at the Black Belt, I thought it was a perfect opportunity to finally get my hands on the tooth. And I was right. I'm sorry I had to smack you around, Jax, but you were definitely in the way."

"How did you find the safe?" Frank asked. "How did you know where it was?"

"It took a while," Nick said. "But I have astute powers of observation. I noticed a small tear in the carpet near the corner of the file cabinet. I took a chance—and there it was."

"Who makes your cross-trainers for you?" Joe asked.

"Jax was right," Nick said. "You two are clever detectives. Yes, it was I who kicked you onto the tracks. I didn't think you'd ever guess that was me. After that buffoon Pierre Castenet made such a scene in the restaurant, I was sure you'd blame him. Apparently I made a mistake on that one."

"Oh, you've made a lot of mistakes," Officer Somerset said. He and a couple of his colleagues walked up to them. "Thank you, gentlemen, for all your help. You've certainly been making my job easier the last few days."

Frank removed the antique cuffs, and Officer

Somerset put official cuffs on Nick's wrists. The culprit was thoroughly frisked, but the tooth was not found.

"Don't worry," Officer Somerset said as Nick was being taken away. "We'll make him talk. That is, of course, if it isn't too late and the Molar Mike is already in the global marketplace."

"I don't think it is," Frank said. "He told us what he planned to do with it, and it sounded like he hadn't done it yet. I might even know where the tooth is. Can you get us into the Tower of London?"

"Right now?" the police officer asked.

"Yes," Jax pleaded. "If Frank thinks he knows where it is, I believe him."

"Yes—let's go," Joe said. "Jax, all you have to do is boot up the program for the Molar Mike and broadcast to it at full volume. We'll hear the transmission and be able to zero in on the tooth."

"And we might not even have to do that," Frank added mysteriously.

Once again Officer Somerset sent his fellow officers off with a Hardy capture. Jax and Joe gathered up all the props they'd used to trap Nick, and all four of them left in Officer Somerset's car.

Once inside the Tower of London, Frank led his party and a Tower night guard to Nick's space in the employees' building. The guard opened the door to Nick's chaotic workplace.

"Nick has a major ego," Frank reasoned. "He

likes to brag about his skills and accomplishments. So I asked myself, if I were Nick, where would I put the most valuable tooth in the world?" He walked toward the table beneath the window.

"In my own mouth, of course," Joe said. "Frank, you're a genius!"

Frank went to the burlap-and-plaster model Nick had made of his own head. He pried open the mouth until it split at the corners of the lips. He showed the others a tooth at the back of the upper jaw that stuck out above the others. Jax sighed. It was the Molar Mike.

"I'm sure we'll find all the papers and other materials in here too," Frank said, looking around at the messy room. It may take a week. . . ."

"Mr. Brighton, we wouldn't presume to touch this delicate invention," Officer Somerset said, clearly impressed with the ingenious tooth. "We'll allow you to take this wax head with you and extract the tooth in the appropriate environment—your medical clinic. When we need it for evidence, I'll assume you will bring it to us."

Jax tried to lift the head, but it wouldn't budge off the pedestal that held it—and the pedestal was bolted to the table.

Joe remembered the moment he flew through the air and out onto the Underground tracks. "Allow me," he said. He cradled Nick's burlap head in the crook of his arm and, with one powerful twist, wrenched it off the pedestal and handed it to Jax.

Frank grinned. "One final beheading at the Tower of London!"

NOW ON AUDIO!

The Original HARDY BOYS and NANCY DREW MYSTERIES

Available for the first time
EVER as audiobooks!

Listen to the mysterious adventures of these clever teen detectives.

Nancy Drew® #1:
The Secret of the Old Clock
0-8072-0754-3

The Hardy Boys® #1:
The Tower Treasure
0-8072-0766-7

Nancy Drew® #2:
The Hidden Staircase
0-8072-0757-8

The Hardy Boys® #2:
The House on the Cliff
0-8072-0769-1

Each program: Unabridged • 2 cassettes
$18.00/$28.00C

LISTENING LIBRARY is a registered trademark of Random House, Inc.
Nancy Drew Hardy Boys and all related characters ©® S&S, Inc.

Available wherever books and audiobooks are sold
Log on to www.listeninglibrary.com to listen to audio excerpts from these brain-teasing mysteries.

GREAT MIDDLE-GRADE FICTION FROM
Andrew Clements,
MASTER OF THE SCHOOL STORY

FRINDLE
0-689-80669-8
(hardcover)

0-689-81876-9
(paperback)

THE SCHOOL STORY
0-689-82594-3
(hardcover)

0-689-85186-3
(paperback)

THE LANDRY NEWS
0-689-81817-3
(hardcover)

0-689-82868-3
(paperback)

THE JACKET
0-689-82595-1
(hardcover)

0-689-86010-2
(paperback)

THE JANITOR'S BOY
0-689-81818-1
(hardcover)

0-689-83585-X
(paperback)

A WEEK IN THE WOODS
0-689-82596-X
(hardcover)

0-689-85802-7
(paperback)

"Few contemporary writers portray the public school world better than Clements."—*New York Times Book Review*

ALADDIN PAPERBACKS

New York   London   Toronto   Sydney

www.SimonSaysKids.com

Have you read all of the books in the Harvey Angell trilogy?

Harvey Angell brightens up orphan Henry's life like a supercharged thunderbolt, and nothing will ever be the same again! But Harvey Angell's true identity is a mystery—one that Henry's got to solve!

While on a seaside vacation Henry discovers the ghost of an unhappy girl haunting his rental house. None of the lodgers is going to get any sleep until Henry and Harvey uncover the shocking secrets of Sibbald House.

Henry finds an extraordinary baby hidden in his garden—a baby with tiny antennae instead of eyebrows, and ears that look like buttercups! Henry's running out of time, and he has to find Harvey Angell before this mystery turns into a cosmic disaster.

Aladdin Paperbacks • Simon & Schuster Children's Publishing Division
www.SimonSaysKids.com

She's sharp.

She's smart.

She's confident.

She's unstoppable.

And she's on your trail.

MEET THE NEW NANCY DREW

Still sleuthing,

still solving crimes,

but she's got some new tricks up her sleeve

NANCY
DREW

girl detectiv